PROMISE
OF PARADISE

Karen Lawton Barrett

A KISMET™ Romance

METEOR PUBLISHING CORPORATION
Bensalem, Pennsylvania

To Phillip and Duffy,
I have all I need.

And to Terese, who's grown into
a lovely young woman.

KAREN LAWTON BARRETT

Karen is a big believer in second chances—in life, in friendship, and in love—so that's what she writes about. Her second chance came when she started dating an ex-schoolmate, who informed her he'd had a crush on her in high school. A marriage proposal three weeks after their first date proved this man to be the true romantic she'd been looking for—so she married him. Today, they have a wonderful little boy and live happily in the central California town where they grew up.

Other KISMET books by Karen Lawton Barrett:

No. 20 *CHEATED HEARTS*

ONE

It was a simple, two-line personal ad. She didn't know why she noticed it. She rarely paid attention to the classifieds, and even more rarely read anything other than the garage- and estate-sales sections looking for used books for her shop. But there it was: "E. Pendleton. Imperative you call re grandfather Matt."

The number that followed was local, Eden realized, biting her lip in dismay. She shifted in the huge armchair she kept behind the counter as a million questions filled her mind. Could he really be here in Portland? Unbidden, excitement filled her. After all these years of knowing he was a continent away in Connecticut, Eden could hardly believe her grandfather could be this close.

Eden glanced at the phone which sat barely a foot from her. All she had to do was pick up the receiver and dial. She inched her long body out of the chair and set the newspaper on the polished wood counter. *It wouldn't hurt to find out who the number belongs to,* she told herself out loud. Luckily, there was no one to hear her. Mondays were notoriously slow in the book business, so it was the day off for her two assistants.

Eden drew a deep breath, grabbed the receiver with a shaking hand, and punched out the numbers she'd already memorized. Her heart hammered in her chest, so loud that she barely heard the first ring. The second ring made her slam down the phone. "No! I'm not ready," she whispered. Tears of disappointment formed in her eyes, spilling over to trickle down her cheeks. "Don't you understand? I'm just not ready," she told the black object that seemed to glare at her accusingly.

Brushing away the wetness with an impatient hand, Eden threw herself back into the chair, which felt about as comfortable as a bed of nails. Why did this have to happen now? She thought she'd have months to prepare for this meeting. Her agent had only just started negotiations on the book that was to be the catalyst and the peace offering.

Eden rubbed her temples, trying to prevent the headache that threatened. How could this have happened? Her grandfather must have hired someone to look for her. Eden's hands dropped to her lap as she realized her carefully thought-out plans had been shot to hell by some greedy detective eager to keep earning a generous retainer. It had to be a mistake. There was no way anyone could have found out where she lived.

That was it, she thought, feeling a little more relaxed. It had been a fluke, an accident of fate, a shot in the dark that couldn't possibly hit pay dirt. When she didn't answer the ad, as the detective was sure she would not, he would try something else, somewhere else. Anything to keep the money rolling in. And she could go back to her original plan.

Eden wasn't sure she believed the fantasy she'd just concocted, but it was better than accepting that her grandfather might find her before she had her gift in hand. Determined to put the ad out of her mind, Eden picked up the paperback she'd started yesterday before the shop had gotten so busy. There was nothing like an old mystery to get your mind off things.

Fifteen minutes later the brass bell over the door tinkled the entrance of a customer. Eden tossed the book onto the counter, stood and placed her oversize reading glasses on top of it. She was glad for the interruption, since she hadn't been able to concentrate anyway.

The polite smile she had fixed on her face faded in surprise as Eden took in the man making his way toward her. Oddly enough, her first impression was that he was the warmest-looking person she'd ever seen. She smiled inwardly at the strange thought. What kind of description was that?

Tilting her head, she studied the stranger a little more closely. Eden was tall, almost six feet, but he was taller by at least four inches. Water dripped from his dark-brown hair, which burned with red highlights even through the dampness.

He reached the counter, and Eden nodded. She decided he couldn't be older than thirty-five. His tanned skin glowed with good health, and she found herself immediately liking his face, which sported the creases of someone who laughed easily. Even his green eyes were warm, reminding her of sun-drenched leaves.

She saw the lines around his eyes deepen with amusement and realized she hadn't even bothered to greet him.

"Good morning, sir, may I help you?"

The smile that followed could have made her forget her own name, Eden thought as she fought the urge to return his grin. It was almost irresistible, flirtatious and yet respectful at the same time. She got the idea that like most men he knew his own charm, but somehow she felt this one didn't use it unless absolutely necessary. A more cynical voice interrupted her thoughts. With looks like his, he wouldn't have to, it said. Women probably dropped at his feet.

Discomfited by the conversation going on inside her head, Eden reddened, her embarrassment not helped by the fact that he still hadn't said anything. He just gazed at her with those wonderful green eyes. She shifted uncomfortably under his perusal. What was he staring at? Usually men didn't give her a second glance. She made sure of it. The combination of drab clothes and a hands-off attitude tended to keep unwanted advances at bay.

But this one was not only looking at her. It seemed as if he was actually seeing beneath the forbidding veneer she tried to cultivate. Uneasy that this was more wishful thinking on her part than anything the stranger had actually perceived, Eden stepped back, almost falling over the chair.

Before she could right herself, he was there, grabbing for her arm, helping her to stand up. "Are you all right, miss?"

Eden stared up into his leaf-green eyes that seemed to sparkle with a life of their own. "Yes . . . No . . . I . . ."

His eyes seemed to smile with curiosity and concern. "Well, which is it?"

Eden tore her gaze away, only to have it fall on his mouth. If I say no, will you kiss it better? Appalled, Eden's gaze flew to his face, but his polite expression reassured her she hadn't asked the question aloud.

Eden pulled away from his disconcerting touch. "I'm fine," she said abruptly, only just remembering to add, "Thank you."

Standing ramrod straight, she put on her best no-

nonsense expression, the one she used for teenage boys who came in asking for dirty books. "Sir, is there something I can do for you?"

He grinned as if enjoying her discomfort. "I'm looking for Aurora Prince. This is the address I was given."

It seemed he had already decided *she* couldn't possibly be the author of those steamy historical romances—especially since she'd acted like some love-starved virgin when he'd merely been preventing a fall.

"Is she expecting you?" The question was unnecessary. She already knew Aurora Prince expected no one.

"No, but I'm sure she'll see me. I'm Gabriel Phillips, from Townsend and Ericsen, her publisher." Confidence filled his voice.

Eden wasn't impressed; ice filled hers. "Then you know that Aurora Prince sees no one. How did you get this address?"

He grinned. "I have my ways."

"I'm sure you do." Maybe that was one of the times he'd found it necessary to use his charm, Eden thought, wondering which of her agent's secretaries had been the lucky recipient. Her agent was a fairly young woman, but she was also ethical. Andrea Jackson would definitely refuse to give out something as personal as an author's address willingly. "Miss Prince is in Europe doing research. She won't be back for months."

Although Gabriel Phillips' face fell in disappointment, his eyes seemed to narrow in doubt. Eden wasn't surprised. Even after years of practice in shading the truth so no one discovered that Eden Pendleton and Aurora Prince were the same person, she still stumbled over any lies. Dane had once told her that her innate honesty shone in her eyes. But being an expert deceiver, her ex-lover wouldn't have known the truth if it hit him in the face.

Focusing on Gabriel's disappointment, curiosity got the better of her. The emotion in his face was far too intense. It was almost as if he had a personal stake in whatever he wanted from Aurora Prince. "Why do you need to see her? No one from Townsend and Ericsen has ever tried to talk about her books in person before. They've all respected her need for privacy."

He regarded her suspiciously. "How do you know?"

"We're good friends," she said. Well, it wasn't really a lie. Her alter ego was her best friend, allowing her to write about her fantasies without her grandfather ever finding out she wrote the very books he'd constantly degraded. "Romantic claptrap," he'd called them. He'd never understood her need for happy endings.

"Then maybe you can give me a phone number where I can reach her?"

"I'm sorry, I can't do that." Why did he sound so urgent? "Maybe if you told me why you need to see her?'' she asked, wondering why she felt a sudden urge to comfort this big man. From the looks of him, he could obviously take care of himself.

He shook his head. "It's personal."

Eden's heart dropped. He was lying. She'd remember if she'd ever met this man before. "If it's important you can get in touch with her through her agent," she said stiffly.

She picked up a pile of recently delivered cookbooks, intending to put them on their proper shelves. Standing close to Gabriel Phillips was much too dangerous, even if he *was* a liar. He reminded her of feelings she'd vowed years ago to forget. She moved away, heading for the cooking section, faltering in her steps when an ache went through her, a need to be held she hadn't felt since Dane had made it clear he had no intention of taking her with him on his fast track to success.

"Wait! I'd like to talk to you."

Eden glanced back at him. "Why?"

He smiled. "Why not?"

His voice flowed out to her like dark wine. His eyes caressed her with green velvet, sending tremors throughout her body.

Eden straightened her shoulders with resolve. It was just another tactic. Dane had been a liar and a flirt, too. He had made her believe he wanted only her for four years. Gabriel Phillips was after Aurora Prince, and if he had to pay a little extra attention to her mousy friend, then that was the price he had to pay.

"You'll have to communicate with Miss Prince through her agent," she repeated firmly.

Eden shoved a book onto the shelf with more force than necessary. Her grandfather, Tommy, Dane. By the third one, she'd learned her lesson. Men were not to be trusted. Even big handsome ones with warm green eyes.

She turned and walked back to the counter, being very careful not to meet those eyes.

"What's your name?"

Eden started at the sound of his voice, so intent had she been on convincing herself that Gabriel was only being friendly in order to get to Aurora Prince. She narrowed her gaze in suspicion. "Why?"

He laughed, causing her heart to flutter in her chest. His laughter was as warm and rich as a newly baked fudge brownie, and just as inviting. "What do you mean, 'Why?'" His expression became conspiratorial. "Is it a secret?" he whispered.

Eden felt her resistance weaken and became even more determined to stand firm. Men took what they wanted—your love, your body—then left. And this man wasn't any different.

The door to the shop opened. Eden looked up and smiled when one of her regular customers walked in. Mrs. Baird tended to be long-winded. Maybe by the time she finished with her, Gabriel Phillips would be gone.

After a brief "get lost" glance at Gabriel, she walked forward to meet her customer. "Good afternoon, Mrs. Baird, have you finished that pile of mysteries already?"

Gabriel watched her move away toward the back of the shop to show the elderly lady her latest shipment of murder and mayhem, wondering why she looked so familiar. He hadn't missed her telling glance, but he decided to ignore it. Somehow he knew she was the key to getting in touch with Aurora Prince. And Aurora Prince was the key to getting in touch with Eden Pendleton. He didn't care if he had to wait through ten customers. He wasn't leaving until he had Aurora Prince's phone number. He'd gotten too close to finding Matthew Pendleton's granddaughter to give up now. Matt was too important to him.

He scowled unseeingly at the shelf of books in front of him. Eden Pendleton had a lot to answer for, leaving her grandfather alone, disappearing without a trace. He had thought the older man would have gotten used to her absence by now. But Matt had looked worse than ever this morning, his depression hanging over him like a cloud.

Gabriel looked back at the lovely iceberg who'd been so unhelpful. Why would she guard Aurora Prince's privacy so fiercely? And what had made such a beautiful woman determined to be so chilly?

And she was beautiful, Gabriel thought, running

his gaze over her, although she seemed to be doing everything she could to hide that beauty. Her dark-blond hair was pulled back in a manner that hid the highlights. And the colors she wore were all wrong for her, the browns and golds in her paisley blouse pulling the roses from her cheeks. Her skirt should have been shorter. If her legs were as long and shapely as he suspected, it was definitely a shame to cover them up with a mid-calf skirt and a pair of boots.

Gabriel shook his head. No, her voice might be as prim as her bun, but she didn't fool him one bit. The sweet smile she'd let slip and the voluptuous body not quite concealed by her overly large blouse indicated a promise of paradise under the arctic ice she'd tried to display.

He wondered at the stroke of luck that had led him straight to this lovely stranger with the rain-colored eyes. Once he found Eden Pendleton for Matt, he was going to spend some time exploring those pools of liquid silver in which he'd willingly drown.

Glancing at the two women discussing the merits of the latest Dick Francis mystery, he decided he might as well relax. She might be determined to draw out her discussion, but if she thought he was going to leave, she had another think coming.

While he waited, Gabriel contented himself with wandering through the heavily laden bookshelves. In spite of the dark, polished mahogany shelves, the profusion of hanging plants and the light from the front window and skylights gave the shop an airy feeling. He knew he could spend hours here, especially when he discovered she sold old and rare used books along with the latest releases.

Sauntering through the art section, Gabriel found a well-thumbed tome on the history of printing and immediately became engrossed in it.

"Why are you still here?"

Gabriel started at the sound of her voice. Deciding to buy the book, he tucked it under his arm and turned to look at the young woman who awaited an answer to her question. Her expression managed to mix uncertainty with bravado, and Gabriel found his heart melting at the sight of it. What idiot had hurt her so much that she couldn't even accept a little attention from an interested admirer?

He smiled. "I was browsing. Besides, you haven't told me your name yet."

He thought he saw a tiny hint of softening in her icy demeanor, but couldn't explain the burst of joy inside him when he was rewarded with a tiny grin.

"It's Eden. Eden Pendleton."

Gabriel, who had been thinking that her smile was as welcome as a rainbow after a storm, stopped to stare. "Did you say Eden Pendleton?" He could hardly believe it. *This* was the young woman for whom he'd been looking for seven years!

"Yes."

"Matthew Pendleton's granddaughter?" Although he felt he had to ask, there was no doubt in his mind.

That was why she had looked familiar. The twenty-eight-year-old who stood in front of him had changed a lot from the seventeen-year-old in the picture he'd carried in his wallet the last seven years, but she was definitely the same girl. And now he'd finally found her. He couldn't wait to see the look on Matt's face when he told him.

Even in his elation he saw Eden's expression change briefly to one of surprise before turning to one of distrust. "Do you know my grandfather?"

To Gabriel's dismay, her prim tone had returned. Surely she couldn't still be holding a grudge after all this time. She wouldn't refuse to see him, would she?

Taking in her uneasy expression, Gabriel decided to give her the benefit of the doubt. She hadn't refused yet.

"Matt Pendleton saved my life. In return, I offered to find his granddaughter for him. I've been looking for you for years."

In spite of his good intentions, Gabriel hadn't been able to keep the accusation out of his voice. He could have kicked himself when she turned away. He'd known this situation had to be handled delicately. She hadn't left her grandfather for a lark. Although Matt had never told him the reason for the split, he'd made it clear that he considered himself at fault.

"You must not have looked very hard," Eden said from behind the counter. "Will that be cash or charge?"

In spite of the underlying sorrow he sensed, Gabriel was irritated by her efforts to change the subject. She hadn't even asked about her grandfather! "Cash. And that's not true. I, and several detectives, searched high and low. But for an eighteen-year-old, you were very clever. You covered your tracks like a pro." He couldn't help feeling a spark of admiration for her ingenuity. It must have taken a lot of courage to cut herself off from the only family she had left.

He caught sight of the newspaper she'd been reading earlier, opened to the personal ads. "And you never answered the ads, did you?"

Eden, who had picked up the thick volume and was looking for the price, glanced up. "Ads? That was the only one I've seen."

"Then you never answered that one." If she had, she wouldn't have been so surprised that he was looking for her. Her grandfather would have answered the phone.

"There was only one person who would even think to look for me, and I had no intention of ever seeing him again."

"Had?" Gabriel suspected the past tense was unintentional and felt his spirits lift. Maybe this wouldn't be so hard after all. "Does that mean you'll see him?"

Eden shook her head. "I can't."

TWO

"What do you mean, you can't? He's your grandfather!"

Tears formed at his outraged tone. Eden brushed them away impatiently. He couldn't possibly understand the soul-searching she'd gone through to reach the point where she could even think of seeing her grandfather.

"I mean, I can't," she repeated firmly. Not now, she cried inwardly. Not yet. She wasn't ready. Oh, why did he have to come along and mess up her plans?

"I can't believe this," Gabriel muttered.

Eden glanced at his face. He seemed so furious. He and her grandfather must have been awfully close for him to react so strongly. Too close for her to

21

trust him with her reasons for waiting. But she might not have a choice. "Are you going to tell him you found me?"

He glared at her as if she'd lost her mind. "Of course I'm going to tell him! He has no idea whether you're alive or dead, and it's killing him!"

Of course he would tell. How could she have expected otherwise? She would do well to remember that Gabriel was her grandfather's friend, and, therefore, not to be trusted. She lifted her chin with pride. "Then tell him I don't want him here." Instantly she wished she could take back the words. That wasn't what she'd meant to say.

"No. That I won't do," he said firmly, his expression now hard and inflexible.

Eden's chin inched up another notch. Gabriel Phillips knew nothing about her, or about the hell her grandfather had put her through with his coldness. He couldn't begin to imagine her need to go to her grandfather with her new book in hand. He would have hated her historicals. Matthew Pendleton read nothing but nonfiction. But because *Serena's Lullaby* was inspired by her grandmother, she was sure it would make him proud. After all these years he would finally approve of her, and maybe give her the love she'd longed for since the age of fourteen.

Eden watched Gabriel pace restlessly. Gathering forces, she surmised. Something he'd said earlier niggled at her brain. Matthew Pendleton had saved his life. She couldn't image her grandfather putting himself out that much for anyone.

"Eden . . ."

Or maybe she could, she thought, remembering a happier time. Before her grandmother had died. Before her parents had been killed. Before he'd turned into the cold, uncaring man who'd driven away his only granddaughter.

"Your grandfather . . ."

She shifted her attention back to the big, handsome man to whom she'd been so attracted, reluctantly noticing the way his tweed sportcoat hugged his wide shoulders over his brown cotton turtleneck. With his close-fitting faded jeans, he looked very much the northwesterner. Not at all the sophisticated man from the East Coast.

She'd be willing to bet the women in New York were crazy about him. And here she'd almost been ready to believe that he might be interested in *her*. When would she ever learn to listen to her brain and not her heart? Men couldn't be trusted. Now that Gabriel Phillips had found Matt Pendleton's granddaughter, he would tell her grandfather his mission had been accomplished and disappear out of her life as quickly as he had appeared.

The thought that he might have become a friend was firmly squelched.

". . . cane."

Eden had missed what Gabriel said, so deep had

she been in her thoughts. But it didn't matter. "Look, Mr. Phillips, I think it's time you left."

Sparks shot from his eyes. "Didn't you hear what I said?"

"Nothing you have to say about my grandfather interests me." Actually, she thought as she put his purchase in a bag, *everything* he had to say about her grandfather interested her. But if she let that interest show, he might just talk her into seeing him. And that could be disastrous. "That will be nineteen dollars and fifty-five cents."

With a frustrated sigh, he handed her a twenty-dollar bill.

Eden gave him his change and his package. "I hope you enjoy the book. Now, if you'll excuse me, I have work to do."

Gabriel slammed the bag down on the counter. "No, I won't excuse you. Your grandfather is an ailing old man. What kind of cold-hearted bitch are you not to care what happens to him?"

Eden stared into the distance, willing herself not to react to his words. Six years ago she had left San Diego and moved to Portland to start a new life. After Dane had dumped her so suddenly she'd wanted nothing to do with her past, including her grandfather. It had never occurred to her that he would become ill.

She focused on Gabriel Phillips' accusing expression. "I'm sorry to hear that. Is . . ."

"You should be!"

Eden's head jerked at his vehement exclamation. "Excuse me?" she asked coldly.

"I said you should be sorry, because he suffered the stroke on the same day I had to tell him there was no trace of you after your graduation from San Diego State."

His words stabbed into her heart like a knife, but she had no intention of letting her pain show. She had been fourteen years old when her parents died, leaving her to live with Matthew Pendleton. And in spite of her grief, she had been glad to go to the grandfather she'd loved so fiercely. But he had rejected her time and again, causing her love to shrivel into a tiny corner of her heart.

And now this stranger was telling her it was *her* fault that Matthew Pendleton had suffered a stroke? "Just who do you think you are, blaming me for my grandfather's illness?" she demanded. "It takes a lot more than bad news to cause a stroke."

"The man's your grandfather, for God's sake. You still should have been with him, no matter what happened between you!" Gabriel was taken aback by his own vehemence. It had been a long time since he'd yelled at someone like this. And after he'd just decided that this situation called for a delicate hand, he'd actually inferred the stroke was her fault. He'd let her damn coldness get to him and blamed Matt's illness on her. Well, so what, he thought as he studied the arctic fire that burned in Eden's eyes.

"How can you say that? You have no idea what

went on between us. Or did my grandfather let you in on all the juicy details?''

He gazed at Eden's face. Even in anger it was quite lovely. Her fury had brought roses to her cheeks and sparkle to her eyes. He'd carried a picture of the seventeen-year-old Eden in his wallet since Matt had asked him to help in the search seven years ago. But the girl in the picture had been smiling, while the woman who stood before him looked as if she hadn't really smiled in years, except for that one smile she'd bestowed on him earlier. No wonder he hadn't recognized her. What had happened to that girl?

Compassion filled him. Beneath the still waters of Eden's rain-colored eyes lay a world of grief and pain that he longed to erase. It must have been devastating for her to lose her parents at such a young age and then to have a break with her grandfather barely four years later. ''Look, I'm sorry I implied Matt's stroke was your fault, especially since I know he's had high blood pressure for a long time. But I don't understand how you can be so uncaring that you've never gotten in touch with him in the last ten years.''

''Ask my grandfather.''

Once again she turned from him, as if her face might reveal a secret she was determined to keep. He let out a sigh of frustration. ''I have. He said he thinks he hurt you badly.''

She laughed hollowly. ''He *thinks*?''

''By the time I got back from Europe, you'd

already been gone four years. Four years he spent killing himself with work. All he would tell me was he couldn't rest until you had been found. Every spare moment for the next year I spent following every lead the detectives had been able to come up with.''

"And that led you to California?"

Gabriel hid a smile at Eden's open curiosity. So the iceberg begins to thaw, he thought. Maybe this would work out after all. If he tread carefully. "Actually, that was a hunch. I found out your mother was raised in San Diego and figured you might have decided to look for some family connection.''

He raised his eyebrows in question and was glad when she confirmed his theory.

"I did, but all my relatives were dead.''

"Except for your grandfather.''

She winced when his gentle probe hit its mark. "For a long time I considered him dead, too.''

Angry at her denial of the man who had meant so much to him, Gabriel completely missed the implication of her statement. He strode around the counter. When she tried to back away, he grabbed her arms, gently shaking her. "But he's not dead! Not yet. But he could be if he doesn't see his long-lost granddaughter soon.'' He ignored her gasp and her efforts to pull away. "Matt's health has been deteriorating because he's been so depressed. He needs to make peace with the past. Finding you is just what he needs to get a new lease on life. He'll be thrilled to know you're alive and well and living in Portland."

Tears welled in Eden's eyes as the need to be held returned full force. It had been so long since she'd felt the sensations caused by a man's hands. Long, lonely years spent locked up in a cage of her own making. She hardly knew how to react. All the time she tried to pull away, she longed to relax into those strong arms, releasing herself to their comfort.

This was all too much. First, she becomes attracted to a virtual stranger who is flirting with her to get to Aurora Prince. Then, it turns out it is she he's been looking for all along, but only as a favor for her grandfather. If she let Gabriel feel her attraction, it would only embarrass them both.

She jerked away, quickly putting a safe distance between them. "Then why don't you go and tell him!" she cried. Her hands flew to her lips. What was she saying? She didn't want her grandfather told yet.

"No."

Eden gazed at Gabriel's baffling expression. If she searched all the words in her extensive vocabulary, she knew she would never find one to describe the look on his face. Was he really offering her more time? "What do you mean, 'No'?"

"I think you should tell him."

Eden closed her eyes briefly. Had he guessed that was her plan all along? That wouldn't do at all. "Why would I do that?"

He cocked his head to one side, studying Eden as if she was a strange bug under a microscope. She shifted uneasily under his scrutiny. A seemingly satisfied expression came to his face. "Because I think you want to see him, that you know it's time you quit running away."

"I'm not running away," she protested, even as she admitted the truth to herself. She was afraid to face her grandfather, afraid that she'd see the same expression of disapproval and disappointment in his eyes. Once she had the book, it would be different.

"Yes, you are, Eden. Something happened years ago that you felt you couldn't fight, so you ran."

Eden stared at him in awe. Had he read her mind, her soul? How could he possibly know the pain and frustration that had caused her to carefully plan her escape from what seemed an insurmountable situation.

She shook her head to clear it. The fact was he couldn't. He was just guessing. Trying to manipulate her into doing what *he* wanted. He didn't care one bit about *her*.

She held her head up, determined to withstand Gabriel Phillips' charm. "If you want my grandfather to know, you'll have to tell him. I've made my own life here and have no intention of bringing back the past." *At least, not until I'm sure I can handle it,* she added silently.

Eden stood her ground when Gabriel moved closer, then wished she hadn't when he reached out his hand to touch her cheek. His tender caress made her want to cry.

"Sometimes, Eden, we have to bring back the past in order to truly enjoy the future."

His statement had come so close to what she herself had decided a year ago that Eden felt as if her soul had been cut open and exposed. For five years she'd lived just fine with her store and her fantasies. Her writing had given her all the excitement she needed, with none of the hurt that came with reality.

Then she'd had that dream about her grandmother Serena, and the emptiness had hit her. That was when she'd begun the book. At first she had written it only for herself. Then Andrea had convinced her to have it published. And finally she'd realized that she'd planned it all along as a peace offering to her grandfather. Maybe once he realized that Serena was a big part of Eden, he would no longer disapprove of his granddaughter.

Realizing Gabriel's gentle fingers still stroked her cheek, she stepped back, then closed her eyes against the surprising sensation of being abandoned in spite of the fact that it was she who had broken the contact. That this sensation had appeared after so brief an acquaintance increased her determination to get rid of Gabriel Phillips as soon as possible.

"I'm sorry you've been put to so much trouble, Mr. Phillips, but I have no intention of bringing back the past *or* seeing my grandfather right now. So you might as well leave."

Proud of her cool delivery, she turned to walk away, only to be stopped by his hand on her arm. "What is your problem, Miss Pendleton?"

She stared up at him with wide, innocent eyes. "I beg your pardon?"

"I beg your pardon," he mimicked. "You're so cool! So your grandfather hurt you. He's been trying to find you, to make everything up to you for years. Haven't you ever made a mistake?"

Eden jerked her arm away. "I've made plenty. That's why I refuse to make another one." She wasn't sure if she meant seeing her grandfather or caring about Gabriel Phillips, but it didn't matter. She couldn't see either doing her any good.

"Your grandfather loves you!"

"How do you know?"

"Because I've spent night after night listening to him talk about his beautiful Eden, wondering where you were, terrified that he might never see you again, that you might be dead!"

Eden felt her cheeks heat with indignation. "You have no right to judge me!" She'd had the best of reasons for leaving her grandfather's house, and no stranger was going to make her feel guilty for it.

"Don't I? I care about Matt."

She didn't miss the censure in his voice, but she'd be damned if she would let him push her into seeing her grandfather before she was ready. She wanted their relationship to work this time.

Again she remembered what he'd said earlier

about Matt Pendleton saving his life. "You must know my grandfather very well."

Gabriel wasn't sure he liked being sidetracked, but he knew sometimes you had to give answers in order to get them.

"Matt was my grandfather's best friend. In fact, they lived next door to each other. I spent most of my life in boarding schools, but every July I was sent to Connecticut to stay with my grandfather.

"When I was thirteen, he died. I was devastated. My father and I had never gotten along anyway, and I resented having to spend the summer with him in Oregon." Seeing the interested look on Eden's face, Gabriel decided he was right to cool his approach. After all, he was a stranger, and her hated grandfather's friend; why should she trust him?

"I'm not trying to sound melodramatic, but I got in with a bad group of kids. I could have gotten into real trouble, but Matt happened to visit around that time. Seeing how unhappy I was, he offered to take me back to Connecticut with him. After that, he sort of took over where my grandfather left off." He smiled, remembering the next four summers and the countless weekends he and Matt had spent together. "He even taught me to fish."

A wave of resentment washed over Eden. Her grandfather taught him to fish! What she would have given for that kind of attention. But all he'd ever done was ask how she was doing in school and tell her when he thought she was dressed inappropriately, which was all the time, the way she'd been built. At fourteen, she'd had the body of a twenty-year-old.

Suddenly she couldn't stand to hear another word of praise for her grandfather. She'd loved him so much. Needed him. She still did. But she would never get the kind of approval she wanted until she showed him she could do something to make him proud. When *Serena's Lullaby* was published, she would go see him. Not before.

"I want you to leave, Mr. Phillips."

He looked at her in surprise. "What's wrong?"

She shook her head. "Nothing's wrong." In spite of her denial, she couldn't help feeling that Gabriel Phillips had stolen something from her and she resented him. "Not that I owe you any explanation, but I just don't want to hear any more about my wonderful grandfather. We obviously know two different people. I have to close the shop for lunch now."

"Lunch? *Lunch?* Your grandfather could be dying, and all you care about is eating? You're nothing but a cold, heartless bitch," he ground out, eyes filled with cold fury.

Eden clamped her jaw tight to keep herself from protesting. If he thought she could harm her grandfather's health by her uncaring attitude, then he'd be less inclined to tell Matt of her presence in Portland.

At her silence, she watched Gabriel's fury turn to icy determination. "I won't give up on this, you frigid little witch. There has to be some feeling left in that lump of ice you call a heart.''

In spite of the fact that she'd deliberately led him to the conclusions he'd reached, Eden couldn't help wishing he could see her as she really was. Maybe a little scared, but definitely not unfeeling. If he knew the warmth that had coursed through her veins at his touch. If he knew the heartache she felt at hearing about her grandfather's illness. If he knew . . .

Then he would be able to put her on a plane to Connecticut within the hour, with no book, with no peace offering, with nothing to give but herself. The very self her grandfather had rejected all those years ago. It wasn't enough.

She stared at him, her expression carefully frozen.

With a disgusted gesture, Gabriel Phillips picked up his bag. He turned back as if wanting to say something, changed his mind, and stalked to the door and left.

Eden let out the breath she'd been holding. Her face felt stiff, as if it really had been frozen. She didn't know when, but he'd be back. And she had better be prepared.

She walked to the phone. The first thing she'd do was check on her agent's progress with *Serena's Lullaby*. The sooner it was published, the better off she'd be.

THREE

Gabriel picked up the receiver of the pay phone with every intention of telling Matt Pendleton that he'd found his granddaughter. But the minute he heard the voice roughened by too many years of smoking cigars, he knew he couldn't. He couldn't be sure how Eden Pendleton would react to a forced meeting, and he couldn't take the chance that she would upset Matt any more than he was already.

After a brief conversation, Gabriel hung up. His gaze fell on Eden's bookstore nearly a block away. He had to convince her to see her grandfather. But right now he was so furious he knew he'd say the wrong thing, maybe alienating her for good, if he hadn't already. And that was a chance he couldn't take.

Trying to calm himself, Gabriel drew a deep breath of cool spring air. Nothing smelled so fresh as Portland after a rain. Lord, he'd missed it. He looked around. Now that the rain had stopped, the sun peeked through the scattering clouds, shining down on the small park across the street. It looked an inviting place to spend a spare half hour. Between looking after his old friend and getting acquainted with his new business, he'd hardly had a chance to sit down these last few days, much less relax.

Maybe after a short walk he'd be refreshed enough to face the ice lady again. In spite of his anger at her obstinacy, he couldn't help being intrigued by Eden Pendleton. She was nothing like the women he knew, to whom any man over the age of eighteen was worthy of sexual advance. None of them had ever fought so hard to get *out* of his arms. As he crossed the street, he wondered if Eden Pendleton ever thawed out long enough to spend some time in the park or if she just holed up in her store all the time.

Gabriel wandered through the park, stopping at the well-tended rose garden. The warming rays brought out the sweet fragrance of the flowers, something he had missed greatly in the last few years he had lived away from Portland. But now that he had returned to the City of Roses, he would savor it.

He bent to breathe in the scent of a pale-pink bud. When was the last time Eden Pendleton was sent roses? Did she even date, he thought, or was that hands-off attitude of hers meant to scare men away? He wondered what she'd think if she knew it only made him *more* interested. With that face and figure, there had to be something more under her drab clothes. He couldn't believe ice water ran in the veins of a body so clearly meant for love.

And wouldn't you like to be the one to find out? he asked himself as he continued on his walk.

After a few minutes he stopped and sat down on a bench beside some fragrant-smelling shrubs he couldn't find a name for. But the scent was familiar. He spread his legs out and listened to the quiet, happy he had the park to himself. Suddenly, a movement caught his eye.

He gazed down the path, trying to identify the intruder. It was a woman, he knew, dressed in a loosely belted oversize trench coat. It took him a moment to recognize Eden. "So, she does come out of her ice cave once in a while," he muttered to himself.

Gabriel, relieved she hadn't noticed him, watched her move closer. Her hair still pulled back in that awful bun, she carried a newspaper under one arm. She had something in her other hand, but he couldn't see it from this angle.

He half-smiled when she sailed by, eyes front. Heaven forbid she should unwind enough to look around, he thought. But he couldn't help admiring the way she carried herself, head high, back straight. Stately, like a clipper ship, yet fluidly, like a dancer. This was not a woman who would back away from a fight. So why had she run away from her grandfather?

He watched as she walked to a bench not far from him, just across from a small grove of bare-branched fruit trees just beginning to sprout buds. Instead of reading the paper, as he thought she'd do, she placed it on the wet bench and sat on it, which enabled him to see the item she held in her hand. An ice-cream cone! A double decker and probably strawberry, judging from its color. Switching the cone from one hand to the other, she managed to shed her coat.

"Eden Pendleton with an ice-cream cone. Well, I'll be," he murmured.

His fascination grew as he observed the transformation taking place before him. Holding her cone carefully in one hand, she reached back with the other and took out what he supposed was a bobby pin, laying it on the bench. One after another, she removed several pins, until finally her hair was released from its confining bun.

Involuntarily, Gabriel held his breath as she ran her fingers through her locks, until they fell in a wavy curtain, the sun turning the tarnished dark blond into glowing gold, as thick and smooth as honey.

Releasing the air from his lungs, Gabriel watched as she licked her dripping ice cream then unbuttoned the top few buttons of her blouse, revealing the cleavage between her full breasts.

Gabriel bit his lower lip, as engrossed by the absolute innocence of her movements as by her continuing metamorphosis. It wasn't just that she had no idea she was being watched. It was as if she had no idea that anyone *would* be watching.

Between savoring licks of her cone, she rolled up her sleeves, then proceeded to unfasten the buttons on the front of her skirt to the middle of her thigh. Having only one hand to work with caused her to move slowly, making her actions provocative.

Gabriel ran his gaze over Eden's face, which became younger-looking and more relaxed with each movement. Any doubt that her strip tease was meant to tantalize flew from his mind. She looked more like a young girl shedding her confining school clothes than a temptress in a strip joint. He shook his head. What had made her so inhibited that she insisted on covering that glorious body from neck to toe, except in her most private moments.

Gabriel watched as she crossed one long, shapely leg over the other and leaned back, raising her lovely face to the sun's rays. She paused for a moment, absorbing the warmth, then once again brought the cone to her lips and began to lick the melting pink ice cream.

In spite of his confidence that her movements were entirely innocent, Gabriel could no longer see her as a schoolgirl as she turned the cone in her hand, never lifting her tongue from the frozen treat. Her enjoyment shone from her face when she took a bite. It was too much, and the top scoop started to slip,

When she caught it with her other hand, Gabriel let out a sigh of relief, all the time wondering why it should matter. And yet he couldn't force his eyes away from the woman who sucked at the strawberry cream that remained on her long, slim fingers.

Gabriel sat very still, fascination and intrigue mixing with attraction for this surprising woman. He considered going up to her. But his earlier encounter told him that she would be appalled to find her secret transformation had been witnessed by a virtual stranger, especially one who was so close to her grandfather.

He sighed regretfully as her rosy tongue darted out to catch a wayward drip. After years of dating the worldy, sophisticated women he met in New York, it would be nice to get to know a woman who combined innocence and sensuousness with such perfection. But a wall stood between them. She wouldn't dare trust the man who was trying to get her back together with her grandfather. He wasn't sure she trusted any man, and he wondered what had happened to cause this lovely creature to close herself off to being loved.

When she began to nibble on the cone, he knew it was time to leave. He glanced at his watch. Twelve-thirty. She would be reopening her shop soon, and he didn't think it would help her disposition any to find him observing an Eden she obviously wanted to keep hidden.

He stood and walked away, feeling much better than he had an hour ago. Now he knew for sure that Eden Pendleton wasn't the iceberg she tried to be, his hope had been renewed. Matt Pendleton *would* have his granddaughter back.

Eden popped the last bit of cone into her mouth and stood. Eating an ice-cream cone was like meditation to her. While she was licking the frozen cream, she could put everything out of her mind. But once it was gone, reality intruded.

When Gabriel Phillips left, she been in such a state that she knew a cone would be the only thing that would relax her enough to think. After her phone call to her agent, she'd locked up and headed for Swensen's Ice Cream Parlor.

At least that phone call had provided good news, Eden thought as she put on her coat. She picked up the pile of bobby pins and slipped them into her pocket. Andrea had submitted her manuscript to North Star Publishing, who had been very interested. They'd discussed the company's offer, and Eden had given Andrea the go ahead. The truth was, she probably would have agreed no matter what the offer. But she felt lucky that the book was going to such a prestigious company.

She picked up the newspaper on which she'd been sitting and frowned. She hadn't counted on her grandfather being ill, she thought as she walked back to the shop. He'd seemed so strong, so formidable, all those years ago. Of course, that strength might have been the problem, since it seemed he'd kept his emotions so bottled up that he'd developed high blood pressure.

Gabriel Phillips thought she was being heartless, refusing to see her grandfather. But Matt's ill health was one of the reasons she wanted to wait. She had no idea what she was going to say to him once they met. What if she blew up? What if they fought? Wouldn't that be worse for his health than not knowing where she was?

She stopped and searched her pockets for the key to her store. As she fit her key into the lock, it occurred to her that her grandfather might already know. She wouldn't be surprised if Gabriel had gone to the nearest phone to call him. She pushed open the door with more force than necessary. Damn! How was she going to put off seeing him if he knew where to find her?

Eden locked the door and made her way to the back office. Even if Gabriel had told him, her grandfather wouldn't be able to get here from Connecticut until tomorrow, but she suspected that Gabriel Phillips wouldn't wait that long before he came back. She took off her coat, removed the bobby pins from the pocket, and walked into the bathroom. It was time to replace the armor.

Picking up a brush, Eden gazed at her reflection

in the mirror. For the first time in six years, she regretted having to put her hair up. She liked it down around her face. It made her feel freer, younger. And she liked pretty clothes and high heels. Her femininity shuddered at the thought of donning unflattering browns and beiges that pulled the color from her face.

Eden remembered the strange look on Gabriel Phillips face and scowled. It was almost as if he'd seen through the wall she'd tried to erect—something no man had done since she'd developed an attitude of disdain toward men.

It was her interest in him that had drawn Dane Martens to her. It was her beauty that had kept him there. She hadn't realized until the end that living with her had given him the prestige he craved. His friends had looked up to him for "owning" the most beautiful girl on campus.

But the very thing that gave him status in college was the thing he felt would hold him back in the real world. "I'm on the fast track, honey, and you're just too beautiful to be a corporate wife. All the other wives would be jealous," he'd told her the day after graduation.

As if punishing herself for her thoughts, Eden pulled back her hair, uncaring that the pins stuck her scalp. How would Gabriel Phillips react to Eden Pendleton in full feather? Would he want her? Or would he see it as a crack in her armor, as something to use to get her to go to her grandfather?

She pushed in the last pin and buttoned up her blouse. What did it matter? He wasn't going to see her like that. She knew from experience that letting up on her wardrobe meant letting go of her control. And it seemed she'd let go of too much already.

Yesterday it would never have occurred to her to wonder how a man would react to her without her boring clothes. She'd been content with her shop and her writing. Her only need had been to make peace with her grandfather.

The minute Gabriel Phillips walked into her shop everything began to change. She was no longer in charge of her fate. One phone call from him could ruin everything.

Dodging raindrops and puddles, Gabriel made his way down the street. The transformation he'd witnessed in the park had served to buoy his confidence. All he had to do was change his tactics. As long as he allowed Eden to remain the ice queen, he didn't have a chance of convincing her to change her mind. But if he coaxed her to shed the ice, to be the warm, sensuous woman he'd seen in the park, he knew she would agree to see Matt and put his mind at rest.

Gabriel smiled at the altruistic turn of his thoughts. Who was he kidding? Yes, he wanted Eden and Matt to reunite, but that wasn't his only reason for wanting to thaw Eden's icy exterior. He wanted to see which was the real Eden. Was the promise of paradise he'd seen just that—a promise easily broken? Or was it a vow to make some lucky man happier than he ever thought he could be?

Well, he knew one thing, he thought, as he reached the store, he wasn't going to wait around to let some other man discover the rose under the snow. This one was his.

FOUR

One look at her told him that plucking this rose would not be easy. Eden's thorns were securely in place. Her hair was pulled back tighter than ever, and her expression was definitely forbidding. If he hadn't known better, he would have sworn he'd been transported from springtime in Portland to winter in Chicago, with the wind chill reading at minus forty.

"Did you call him?" she asked as he walked up to the counter where she stood, back straight, gray eyes stormy.

If he hadn't seen the other Eden, he might have been tempted to keep her in suspense, to punish her for her coldness. But having witnessed her miraculous transformation, it had occurred to him that there might be something else going on here, and he'd never find out what if he alienated her.

He shook his head. "No, I didn't call him."

Her release of breath was almost imperceptible, but because he was studying her so intently, Gabriel saw it, and the relief that flashed across her face.

"Why not?" she asked, her tone almost defensive.

"How could I tell a depressed old man that I found his long-lost granddaughter, but she refused to see him?"

Her brief expression of guilt satisfied him that he'd been on the right track. "I won't wait forever, Eden. Matt's not well. He needs to know that you're all right," he informed her. After a pause, he added, "And *you* have to be the one to tell him."

She shook her head. "I've already told you I can't."

Her words were firm, but her voice wavered, as if she'd wanted to say something entirely different.

"What you haven't told me is why you can't see him."

Far from backing down, she raised her stubborn little chin. "I don't owe you any explanations."

Gabriel smiled. "You remind me of your grandmother when you raise your chin like that."

Eden averted her eyes from his, but not before he caught the glimmer of tears. "So, you knew my grandmother, too?" she asked, her voice breaking at the end.

Gabriel focused on Eden's face, confused by her

vulnerability. "Yes. She was a wonderful woman." He half laughed. "With your grandfather I had to be macho, you know, a man like him. A teenager's pride, I guess. But your grandmother let me be a little boy."

Gabriel stared blindly at a row of books. "One night, soon after my grandfather died, she came into my room and found me crying. She brushed away my tears, held me in her arms, and sang to me." He looked at Eden. "That's how I knew to come here."

Her eyebrows raised in question.

"The lullaby," he said.

"The lullaby?"

"Yes, the lullaby at the end of the book. Handed down from generation to generation of your grandmother's family. No one, except Eden Pendleton, could have given it to Aurora Prince."

Gabriel watched Eden's eyes widen in surprise.

"How did you get that book? Andrea wouldn't have submitted it to Townsend and Ericsen. It isn't suitable for a paperback house."

"I don't . . ." Suddenly it occurred to him that she knew an awful lot about who would be shown Aurora Prince's book. Either they must be very good friends or . . . "What difference does it make to you where the book is published?"

Eden blushed, making him even more curious. Was it just the family lullaby? Or was there some other reason for her strange reaction?

"No difference," she answered a little too quickly before glancing away. "I was just curious."

Gabriel studied her averted face. For someone who professed to be only curious, she was acting very nervous. A thought occurred to him. Yes, it fit. His difficulty in finding her. Her reluctance to put him in touch with the reclusive author. Her transformation in the park. It all fit! He was filled with boyish elation at having figured out her secret. "You're Aurora Prince!"

Gabriel looked at Eden, who watched her shoes as if they would help her figure out what to say. Did she resent his discovery? Would she retreat even further into her schoolmarmish persona now that he knew she was the author of several very hot historical romances? Even more important, did she know he had just taken over the company that had made an offer on *Serena's Lullaby*? From her earlier comment, he'd bet not.

Suddenly the situation seemed even more complicated than ever. If he pushed her too hard, he might lose her for the company, for himself, and, most important, for Matt. He could wait, and his company would survive without her book. But would Matthew Pendleton survive without his granddaughter?

He had a lot of thinking to do. For right now he was having a hard enough time taking in what he'd just learned. "You're Aurora Prince."

Eden nodded. If Gabriel's words had been a question, she might have denied it. But what was the use? Her pseudonym had only been a means of making sure her grandfather didn't find her, and one she had expected to be temporary at most. She'd figured her grandfather's detectives would have caught up with her long ago.

"So, that's how you did it."

Brought back from her thoughts, Eden looked up at Gabriel. "Did what?"

"Disappeared so thoroughly."

Eden half smiled. "A halfway decent detective would have caught up with me long ago."

"And that's what you expected, wasn't it?"

Eden lowered her eyes under Gabriel's intense gaze. "I don't know what you're talking about."

Gabriel shook his head. "I think you do, but we'll talk about it another time."

Eden's heart jumped in her chest. "Another time?" she asked as nonchalantly as she could manage. Did that mean he intended to go on seeing her in spite of her refusal to meet with her grandfather?

He picked up the receiver of the telephone that sat on the counter next to the old-fashioned cash register and held it out to her with a telling raise of his brows. "Are you going to call Matt and tell him you're alive and well?"

Eden looked away from his expectant face to hide her disappointment. *Of course, he was talking about your grandfather, you idiot!* She caught a glimpse of herself in an ornate mirror she'd hung on the wall, an unobtrusive way to keep an eye on the customers.

Eden frowned at her image, regretting for the first time in years her decision to tone down her looks. The colors she wore did nothing for her, and her severe hairstyle made her look gaunt. The strongly defined bones of her face needed a looser style to soften them.

"I take it the answer is no," Gabriel commented as if he'd expected no other answer.

Eden turned to face him. "No, Mr. Phillips, I am not going to call my grandfather."

"I can see you're quite adamant."

Eden studied his expression closely. She wasn't quite sure, but it seemed as if he was laughing at her. "I am," she answered, more tentatively than she'd planned. Damn the man! She might have chosen to look the mouse, but she'd never acted like one before.

"Then we'll leave that discussion to another time," Gabriel said good-naturedly.

"Okay," she replied, happy that he didn't plan to . . . "What discussion? There *is* no discussion." Just who did this man think he was? She'd already told him to tell her grandfather himself. She had no intention of seeing her grandfather until the book was published. And nothing Gabriel said would change her mind.

She watched him make a pretense of studying an old movie poster on the wall. "I *said*, there is no discussion."

"I heard you." He turned to Eden with a grin,

infuriating her all the more. "But we do have something else to talk about."

Eden regarded him with suspicion. Why did he have to be so handsome? So charming? So much! She'd been out of practice fending off unwanted males for a long time. And the main problem with Gabriel Phillips was, he wasn't unwanted! She'd been attracted to him from the moment he walked into her shop, and the intervening hours—was it really hours?—had only served to strengthen that attraction.

A hand waved in front of her face. "Yoo hoo? Where did you go?"

Eden closed her eyes briefly. She had to get a grip on herself. She wasn't an impressionable teenager anymore. "Nowhere. I was just thinking."

"Thinking?" His vaguely sly grin belied his innocent tone. "About what?"

It was almost as if he *knew*, Eden thought. This would never do. "I was wondering what else we had to talk about," she replied firmly.

"The book," he said simply, confusing Eden no end.

"The book?"

"Yes. *Serena's Lullaby.*" His glance was cheerfully admonishing. "Since *you* are Aurora Prince, I don't have to wait until she gets back from Europe to talk to her."

"But I've already told *you* that it's unsuitable for Townsend. *Serena's Lullaby* is—"

"An extraordinarily inspired novel more suited to a small publisher with a reputation for printing exceptional books," he finished for her.

Though flattered by his praise, Eden was puzzled. "How do you know this? I really can't imagine that Andrea would have showed it to your firm." What was going on here? Had he gotten it by accident? And why did he seem totally unaware of the fact that his description put Townsend and Ericsen out of the picture anyway? "Well, if you understand what kind of book this is, surely you must realize it would be no use making an offer." Eden blushed at her seeming lack of modesty. "Why are you making an offer? Your company publishes mass-market paperbacks."

"I don't want it for Townsend and Ericsen."

"You don't?" she asked, suddenly wishing she was the type to keep a bottle of brandy on hand. She felt as if she'd been picked up and placed in the middle of someone else's novel.

"No, my father owns North Star Publishing here in Portland. We could never work together, but now that he's decided to retire, he's turned the company over to me."

Finally, she was beginning to see some light. And she wasn't sure she liked it. "You're running North Star?"

He smiled, somewhat wolfishly. "I take it Andrea didn't tell you when you talked to her."

She shook her head. "No, she didn't."

"Did you approve of the offer? I haven't had a

chance to call her." He gave her a slightly accusing look. "I've been too busy chasing down my friend's granddaughter."

Eden decided to ignore his last statement. "Of course I approved of the offer. It was very generous." She studied him intently. "*Why* was it so generous?"

He smiled. "Surely you know?"

She shook her head. Eden had an idea, but she didn't care for what she was thinking so she decided to let him tell her.

"The book is wonderful. Moving, romantic, heartwarming."

Eden couldn't hide her surprise, and Gabriel laughed. "What did you think? That I was trying to buy off Aurora Prince so she'd tell me where to find you?"

Eden felt the heat rise in her cheeks. There was no use denying it. "The thought did occur to me. So Andrea did give you my address?" she asked, somewhat relieved that he hadn't had to charm a secretary to get it. For some reason, the thought of him using that devastating smile on anyone else gave her a sick feeling in her stomach.

Gabriel laughed. "Are you kidding? I tried everything and she still refused. 'It would be unethical,' she informed me. In the end, I had to resort to trickery."

Eden raised her brows. "What kind of trickery?" And exactly what had "everything" been?

He winked. "I sneaked a peek in your file while she was out of the room. So now that you know how protective your agent is, and how unscrupulous I am, shall we have dinner and discuss the book?"

Dinner with him? She wanted to, but a little voice told her to say no. It was true that he'd seemed to accept her decision about her grandfather, but he'd said himself that he wasn't above resorting to tricks.

Suddenly she felt as if she'd been cast asea by fate. Just yesterday she'd been perfectly happy. She'd taken a new step in her career. Her bookstore was doing fine. She no longer had to deal with lecherous men treating her as if she was a plaything.

Eden shook her head. Who was she kidding? She'd finished *Serena's Lullaby* two months ago and still hadn't come up with an idea for her next book. Although working in the store gave her the opportunity to meet plenty of people, she'd been so reluctant to trust them that the only friends she'd made were her part-time employees. As for men, her strong attraction to Gabriel Phillips, a virtual stranger, told her she might have gone a little bit too far in avoiding them. All the fantasies in the world couldn't make up for the lack of being held and loved.

Loved! a little voice inside her brain exclaimed. *You really are far gone, Eden Pendleton, if you think a man like Gabriel Phillips would fall in love with someone who deliberately makes herself out to be a mouse.*

"Eden? Eden! Are you all right?"

Eden blinked up at the subject of her thoughts. He smiled.

"Where did you go this time?" he asked, his amusement at her distraction clear. "Do you do this often?"

"Do what?"

"Go off to never-never land."

Eden sighed. He couldn't have picked a better description. The chances of him caring about her were as far away as that fictional fairyland.

"So, what time shall I pick you up?"

Gabriel's question jerked her back to reality with a vengeance. Had she agreed to have dinner with him? She'd better start paying more attention. She had a feeling this man could sell her the Brooklyn Bridge without her even realizing it.

"Pick me up for what, Gabriel?"

So, he'd finally got her attention, Gabriel thought. "Why, for dinner, of course, to discuss your book." He'd decided pursuing the book would be the safest course, since it was the least emotional.

"What is there to discuss? You've already given your offer to my agent, and I've agreed to it. She handles the finances."

Gabriel smiled. "It's a good thing, if you blank out like that often."

He watched Eden's mouth snap shut on a quick reply and wondered what she'd been about to say. The woman was a true enigma, and he was going to enjoy getting to know her and all of her secrets.

"Don't worry, it isn't finances that we'll be discussing."

"Oh?"

Uh oh, he thought, Miss Prim is back. "*Serena's Lullaby* is a special book. Your first hardbound. I thought you might want to be involved with production." A thrill of satisfaction went through him at the sparkle of interest that lighted Eden's eyes.

"You mean with the cover design?"

He nodded. "With everything, especially promotion." Seeing a touch of apprehension cross her face, he wondered if he'd made a mistake mentioning promotion so soon. Deciding it was best not to give her too much time to think about it, he continued quickly. "What time does the shop close?"

"At six."

"Good, then I'll pick you up at seven." He walked to the door, then stopped. "Eden, there's a very important question I have to ask you."

He was surprised when she seemed to steel herself, then realized she thought he was referring to her grandfather. Not for the first time, he wondered what could have caused the rift between his old friend and this lovely young woman.

"What do you want to know?" Eden prompted.

This time it was Gabriel who had to force himself back to the present. "Oh! Where do you live?"

Eden laughed, causing Gabriel to feel as if he'd been kicked in the solar plexus. Her laughter tinkled along his spine like a Scott Joplin tune, surprising and delighting him.

"I thought you knew," she said. "The reason this address was in Andrea's file is I live above the shop."

"Oh, then I'll pick you up at seven."

When she didn't answer right away, he held his breath, afraid he'd have to persuade her all over again.

"Okay, Gabriel, I'll see you then," she finally answered. "The entrance to my apartment is around the back of the building."

Taking in her sweet smile, Gabriel said good-bye and walked out the door, feeling as if he was thirteen years old. Something he hadn't felt since . . . well, since he *was* thirteen! But even Emily McRae with her micro minis hadn't been as gorgeous as Eden Pendleton, who he knew possessed movie-star good looks under all that drab armor.

Eden watched Gabriel walk down the street, heartily glad that he wasn't walking out of her life. She knew he had two very good reasons for staying in it: her book and her grandfather. But she couldn't help feeling that he'd be interested even if they didn't have those two things in common. Once again the little voice inside her head asked what a sexy, attractive man like Gabriel Phillips would want with a woman who dressed like a mouse. But this time another, more confident, voice spoke up. She didn't *have* to dress like a mouse, did she?

A half hour before Gabriel was to arrive, Eden wrinkled her nose with disgust as she added another inappropriate dress to the growing pile on her bed. It seemed she *did* have to dress like a mouse. There was nothing in her closet that would project any other image. She sank onto the floor in front of the near-empty closet, pulling her large stuffed skunk into her arms. It had been her last birthday present from her father, who used to call her Stinky when she was being mischievous.

"Dane Martens wasn't the only thing I left behind when I moved from San Diego to Portland, Stinky Too," Eden said, thinking wistfully of the colorful wardrobe she'd donated to the Salvation Army before she left California. "What I wouldn't give for just one bright red scarf right now."

The skunk gave her a blank look.

Eden grimaced. "Don't look at me like that, you know I can't wear the black. It's much too . . . too . . . *much!*"

Stinky Too stared up at her with wide eyes.

Eden shook her head. "I know, I know, if I dress like a mouse, Gabriel will think he can walk over me." The black would give her a little extra confidence. She got the feeling Gabriel saw her as an amusing, slightly eccentric author who didn't know how to deal with the real world. Never-never land, indeed! Well, he would see tonight that she could hold her own.

"But the black?" She wavered a moment.

The skunk didn't say a thing.

"All right. *All right!* You win. I don't have any other choice. It will have to be the black."

Eden set the animal aside and stood. She hadn't wanted to resort to this, but if she wanted to look halfway decent for her date tonight, she had no choice. Date? *This isn't a date,* she admonished herself. *It's a business dinner, and you'd do well to remember that!*

FIVE

Gabriel paced up and down at the bottom of the stairs that led to Eden's apartment, only stopping to kick a stray soda can across the alley. How was he supposed to handle her delicately when he was so angry?

Matt had seemed more depressed than ever this evening, especially when he'd had to tell his friend that he'd made no progress in locating his grand-daughter. He'd hated lying to him, and he'd hated the defeated expression that had come over Matt's face.

Gabriel stopped, lifting his head to stare up at the stars peeking through the sparse cloud cover. "Star light, star bright," he murmured. He wished with all his heart that he had told Matt about the book and the lullaby when he first read it. He wished he'd given him the hope of finding Eden then so he didn't have to withhold it from him now. And he wished that Matt's granddaughter hadn't inherited her grandfather's stubbornness.

On the other hand, he was very grateful for that stubbornness in his friend. Because that was what would keep Matt from giving up, and what would buy him the extra time he needed.

Once again, Gabriel wondered what had caused the rift between Matt and Eden. He'd pressed Matt for the answer earlier, but all he'd said was, "I was a foolish old man."

Gabriel hit the metal banister in frustration. Well, he'd be damned if he was going to accept that answer. If he couldn't get it out of the foolish old man, then he'd get it out of his stubborn young granddaughter. His determination renewed, Gabriel climbed the flight of stairs and pounded on Eden's door.

When the door opened, Gabriel strode into the apartment with barely a glance at the young woman who stood holding it. "Get your coat, Eden, we're going to see your grandfather."

The door slammed shut behind him, and Gabriel winced inwardly. Something about that bang made him suspect ordering Eden around was *not* the way to get her to do something.

Well, this time *he* was going to get his way. He stiffened his spine, turned to look at her, and drew in a sharp breath. Even the transformation he'd witnessed earlier couldn't have prepared him for Eden in full flower. She looked stunning.

His gaze went first to her hair, which was *not* pulled back in a bun. Instead she'd left it unbound, brushed over to one side so it flowed across her shoulder like a golden waterfall.

His attention proceeded to her eyes, brightened by a touch of mascara and what he perceived to be anger. In fact, her expression was livid.

"No, we are not," she enunciated, her stormy eyes flashing.

"He needs you, Eden," he said vaguely, taking in the rest of her appearance. Black was definitely her color. Without being too tight, the long-sleeved, high-necked sheath managed to caress her curves lovingly. God, she was beautiful! This was better than he'd ever dreamed.

A thought struck him. If Eden could soften her style of dress for a business dinner, surely she could soften her attitude toward her grandfather. Maybe wishing on stars worked after all.

But Eden had looked away, so he couldn't see her face. "I needed him, *once*," she said, in a voice that tried to be hard.

Able to detect the hint of vulnerability in her drooping shoulders, Gabriel wasn't fooled. And he wasn't there for her, Gabriel surmised. It still confused him. When his grandfather had died, Matt had gone out of his way to make sure he wasn't alone, yet the granddaughter Matt had raised claimed he had been cold and unfeeling. There had to have been some misunderstanding. And the only way to clear it up was to get the two of them together.

"So you're never going to see him again? You're going to hold a grudge forever?" he accused.

Eden swung around, her chin raised in that endearingly stubborn manner that was becoming all too familiar. "What difference does it make to you?"

Gabriel gritted his teeth in exasperation. "I care about your grandfather. I don't want him to waste away, because he can't make peace with you, okay?"

"If he wants to make peace so badly, why didn't he come looking for me himself?"

Her voice caught, and Gabriel realized that Eden was hurting as badly as Matt. His gratitude and love for his old friend had made it hard to see Eden's side in this situation. Earlier, his instincts had warned him to go slowly, and they'd been right. You didn't mend a ten-year separation in ten minutes.

"I see you have no answer. It seems I'm not as important to my grandfather as you'd like me to believe."

Gabriel took a step toward her. "That's not true. He has no idea where you are. I didn't want to raise his hopes if I couldn't find you."

Eden's eyes widened in surprise. "He doesn't have any idea?"

Gabriel shook his head, curious at the brief expression of joy that crossed her face.

"Then it won't make any difference if I don't go see him right away, will it?"

"It certainly would make a difference! He loves you. He misses you."

Eden made a dismissive gesture. "So, what do you want me to do? Drop everything and get on a plane for Connecticut?"

Gabriel shook his head. "No. I want you to get in my car and go to my house."

Eden's brows lowered in confusion. "Your house?"

Satisfied that things might work out sooner than he planned, Gabriel leaned against the back of her huge overstuffed sofa. "Matt seemed so lost when I told him I was moving to Portland that I asked him to come stay and help me get settled."

Eden stare at him with wide, cloudy-gray eyes. "He's here?"

Gabriel nodded.

"In Portland?"

Gabriel nodded again.

Eden could have punched Gabriel, his expression was so smug, as if he'd accomplished what he'd set out to do. He had no idea of the turmoil rioting within her. He couldn't possibly understand that having her grandfather closer made it harder, not easier.

Eden's hands started to shake. She clasped them together, but it didn't help as the tremors took over her body. She wrapped her arms around her waist, trying to ease the shaking that engulfed her. What was she going to do? She wasn't nearly ready to confront her grandfather yet. And a confrontation was exactly what it would be if she saw him now. She'd have no book to raise her confidence. No peace offering. She started to pace around the room.

But what excuse could she give Gabriel for not seeing Matt? At least when she'd thought he was still in Connecticut she had the excuse—though admittably poor—of distance. But now he was mere miles away.

A myriad of emotions washed over her—anger at Gabriel's pushing, guilt at her cowardice, attraction for a man whose only interest was her grandfather, confusion that that caring was one of the things that attracted her. And regret that she was going to have to back away from that attraction, because if she kept seeing him, Gabriel Phillips could easily talk her into doing something rash.

In the end, she decided the only thing she could do was spur on her own anger in order to offset the attraction. She drew a deep breath, gathering all her acting abilities to the fore.

She glared at Gabriel, who sat, arms crossed, complacently waiting for her agreement. "So, you had no intention of discussing *Serena's Lullaby*. The whole purpose of this dinner date was to bully me into seeing Matt."

Gabriel lowered his arms and slowly stood. His eyes narrowed. "Bully?" he asked, his tone slightly dangerous.

Eden stood her ground, hiding her satisfaction that

he'd taken the bait. "You just can't accept that the decision to see my grandfather belongs to me so you made up this ruse. I should have known."

He strode over to her. "I didn't make up anything!"

Eden laughed and turned away. "I'll bet!"

She walked over to the ornate gilt mirror that hung over her fireplace. The bobby pins she'd taken out earlier still lay on the mantel. She picked one up and started twisting her hair into a bun. "You never had any intention of getting me involved with the book." She stuck the first pin, puncturing her scalp in the process, causing her to wince.

"That's not true!" Gabriel protested.

Eden was determined not to listen. "It *is* true." She thrust in another pin. "In fact, you didn't even plan to take me to dinner."

When he didn't answer right away, Eden snuck a peek at his reaction in the mirror and was immediately confused. He didn't even look angry. Afraid he'd catch her gaze, she returned to her hair.

"It's not going to work, you know," he said softly, as he walked up to stand behind her.

Eden refused to meet his eyes. "I don't know what you're talking about." Damn! It hadn't worked after all.

"Yes, you do." He reached up to release one of the pins.

"Stop that!" She replaced it with another.

"I've already seen you without your armor. Putting it back on isn't going to change a thing.'' He removed two bobby pins.

"I like my hair this way,'' she declared, then made the mistake of looking at his reflection.

He smiled. "No, you don't. You hate having your hair confined. You'd rather leave it unbound, free to fly in the breeze.''

Eden drew a shaky breath. The husky lilt of his voice played across her spine and caused her blood to run like thick honey in her veins. If she could just get him to quit talking, maybe she could resist the allure of his words.

Gabriel's hand brushed across the back of her neck as he removed yet another bobby pin, and Eden knew she was doomed. "Turn around, Eden,'' he ordered and entreated at the same time.

"No,'' she whispered, knowing if she did she would surely be lost forever.

He grasped her shoulders gently and turned her to face him. His face lit with a sweetly sexy smile, he removed the last of the pins. "There,'' he said, gently running his fingers through the golden tresses. "That's how it should be—free and silky and flowing.''

Eden tried to swallow the lump in her throat, but it remained. No man had ever treated her like this. As if she was a fragile creature from a fairy tale who'd disappear at the first harsh word. She stared up into Gabriel's leaf-green eyes, which had softened and deepened, turning them into a sunlit forest full of mystery and promise. "Gabriel?"

He smiled briefly before taking her mouth in a kiss that broke the magic spell and taught her that reality was better than anything she'd ever imagined. His lips invited and demanded her response, taking and giving pleasure, as forceful as a tornado, yet as gentle as a spring rain.

Eden didn't even try to resist. This was what she'd wanted since she first saw his full, firm lips part in a devastating smile. She'd longed for the taste of his kiss, the feel of his mouth on hers, the sensation of his darting tongue. Her hands crept up the nubby tweed of his jacket, glorying in the rough feel of the material against her skin contrasted with the moist smoothness of his tongue as it played with hers.

She loved the firmness of his fingers on her waist. All gentleness was gone. This was a man who wanted a woman, not some fairy-tale princess. Being held in Gabriel's arms was like being held in the eye of a storm, calm and intense, completely aware of the wildness held in check just moments away. And she gave herself up to it, as naturally as the earth yielded to the rain and the trees swayed with the wind.

Gabriel took his mouth from her, pulling her more tightly into his arms. "Eden, Eden, you're so beautiful, so sexy. Don't ever try to hide from me again," he whispered against her hair.

A thrill went through her, no less intense for being

the hundredth or the thousandth since he'd first come into her life. This was what she'd been waiting for. This was what she'd been trying to find with Dane all those years, why she'd let herself be fooled into thinking that Dane loved her.

Loved! Eden balled her fists and pushed against Gabriel. He refused to let her go. She pushed harder. How could she have been so stupid? A man didn't have to love a woman to kiss her. Gabriel had said she was beautiful and sexy, not kind, smart, or anything else that could make her believe that he wanted her, not just her body.

With one final shove, she was out of his arms.

"What's wrong, honey?"

Eden shook her head. There was no way she'd reveal her naiveté to him. He was a sophisticated man of the world. He'd lived in New York City the past few years, in Europe the years before. He'd laugh his head off.

"Nothing's wrong. It's just getting a little too hot in here."

He smiled. "You mean, *we're* getting a little too hot."

Eden blushed.

"Maybe going to dinner will cool the situation a little."

Eden looked at him in confusion. "You want to take me to dinner?"

Gabriel's green eyes flamed. "I want to take you to bed." He grinned. "But I'll settle for dinner."

A hot shudder went through her at the invitation in Gabriel's eyes. The last thing she wanted was food. But she knew the first thing she wanted—to show Gabriel to the bedroom, to take off his clothes, to see if the color of the rest of his body matched the warm glow of his face—was forbidden. It was too soon. He was too soon. How could they build a relationship with the problem of her grandfather standing between them?

She gazed at the big, handsome man who looked at her with an expression of little-boy expectation on his face. She couldn't tell him to go, and she couldn't let him stay.

"Yes," she said, "I think dinner is a good idea."

Actually, she thought after they'd been in the car fifteen minutes, the best idea would have been him going to dinner and her staying home by herself. The masculine, lemony scent of him had overwhelmed her senses to the point where she was ready to slam her foot on the brake and tell him to turn around.

"What made you choose Portland to move to?" Gabriel asked.

The prosaic question startled her out of her erotic thoughts. It took a moment of concentration before she could come up with an answer that had nothing to do with Dane's betrayal. "The weather, mostly," she finally said.

He raised an eyebrow. "You came up here for the

rain? You lived in San Diego, which is supposed to have the most perfect weather on the West Coast."

"All that perfection can get a little boring," she said.

"Right," he said sardonically.

She supposed that did sound a bit ridiculous. San Diego was beautiful. She'd enjoyed every minute she'd lived there, until the last disaster.

"I *was* raised in Connecticut, you know. I missed the different seasons. All us transplanted easterners do." Or at least that's what she'd heard. Personally, she hadn't missed the freezing winters in the least.

"And you thought you'd find seasons up here? Haven't you heard the old joke we Portlanders tell on ourselves?"

She smiled. "You mean the one about Portland having only two seasons?"

He laughed. "Yeah, the rainy one and . . ."

"The other three days!" she finished, and they laughed together. Eden couldn't remember the last time she'd had such an easy conversation with a man.

A man? she thought. What had she been thinking? This wasn't just any casual date, and Gabriel wasn't just any man. He was her grandfather's friend. He was the one who could break the news about her any day now if she couldn't convince him not to.

And more than that. He was the one who had brought sensuality back into her life. When he'd touched her the first time, she wanted to throw herself into his arms. Just having him sitting next to her, smelling so wonderful, laughing in that abandoned way of his made her want to lock him away forever.

So he wouldn't leave her like Dane? a voice said.

No! She couldn't do this. *Gabriel's a stranger, a stranger with a motive for seeing her. I have to stop thinking of him this way.*

She looked over at Gabriel, who had started to sing along to an oldie from the sixties on the radio. He was so handsome, so sexy. *And so dangerous to you, Eden. You can't let him get to you. Do you hear me? You can't!*

SIX

Awaking the next morning from a dream in which she *had* let Gabriel stay, Eden immediately threw back the covers and climbed out of bed. So much for not letting him get to her. It had taken hours for her to fall asleep last night, because she couldn't get that man off her mind. The last thing she needed was to lie around all morning daydreaming about a relationship that might never exist. Especially since there was a distinct possibility that there was a purpose behind all that charm, that purpose being convincing her to see her grandfather, in spite of the fact he hadn't mentioned Matt the whole time they had been out last night.

But there was no denying it, Eden thought as she walked into the bathroom to splash cold water on her face, Gabriel Phillips was definitely charming. And sexy! Even after the stern talk she'd had with herself, the feelings she'd had in the car hadn't diminished once they'd arrived at the restaurant. In fact, they'd gotten worse!

Even now, she could feel the electric shock that had coursed through her when he had rubbed his thumb along the pulse of her wrist or "accidentally" bumped her knee. She'd never been so sexually attracted to a man in her life. Even Dane's expert lovemaking hadn't aroused the sensations that merely staring into Gabriel's warm green eyes caused.

Enough, Eden! It's time to get to work, she admonished herself as she pulled on brown cords and a heavy gold sweater. She'd promised herself, around three A.M., that first thing this morning she'd start outlining a new book. If that couldn't take her mind off the sexy green light that shined from Gabriel's eyes, nothing could! There was nothing like plotting a new book to monopolize your concentration.

Eden plopped onto her desk chair and pressed the power button on her computer. Since she had no title in mind, she opened a file called "New Book." A blank screen appeared before her eyes.

An hour later, it was still there.

Eden stared at it in dismay. During the last sixty minutes, she had made her bed, fixed and eaten breakfast, washed the dishes, dusted *and* vacuumed the entire apartment, but she hadn't typed anything into her computer. Nothing had come to her. Not one idea. Not one sentence. Not one word! Now what was she supposed to do?

Unable to sit, Eden jumped up and started pacing. She couldn't believe this was happening. She'd never had writer's block before. Of course, she hadn't had so much going on in her life before, either: her estranged grandfather just a few miles away and a handsome man looking at her as if she was the greatest thing since sliced bread.

"This is awful! Now, I'm thinking in clichés," she said to her reflection in the mirror. "Oh, well, you know what they say, 'When the going gets tough, the tough . . .'" Eden paused as she really looked at herself. "Go shopping?"

Eden walked over and turned off the computer. The more she thought about the idea, the more she liked it. God, she was tired of looking like a frump. She'd felt really good last night, all dressed up. It had given her a confidence she hadn't felt in years. Which was pretty funny when she thought about the fact that she'd worn the drab clothes to give her the very assurance she hadn't felt until she'd shed them.

Yes, she definitely needed a different style. She wouldn't need to buy very much, just a few bright blouses, maybe a couple of printed scarves for her hair. She'd felt totally inadequate dealing with Gabriel's charm yesterday. Maybe some new clothes would help her keep the extra confidence the black dress had conjured.

Several hours later, Eden made her way down the street, her arms laden with packages. A bag slipped from her grasp, and Eden stopped briefly to retrieve it. What had started out as a shopping trip to pick up a few things had turned into a full-blown shopping spree. Eden laughed a little at herself. If she'd known she was going to go crazy, she would have taken her car.

Eden stopped at a corner and rearranged her packages while she waited for the Walk signal. Gabriel had said he would call today to make arrangements for them to discuss her book. And she was sure he'd ask her about seeing her grandfather again. He cared too much about Matt to let up on her. When that time came, she would need all the strength and spirit she could muster. Oh, well, if these clothes didn't do the trick, nothing would, she thought.

Eden crossed the street, happy to see the bookshop less than a block away. She didn't know how much longer her arms could hold out. It was funny. At the time, she didn't realize she was buying out the store. No wonder the salesclerks had been smiling ear to ear. They probably worked on commission.

Eden considered going around to the back entrance so she wouldn't have to face her assistants. She hadn't been able to resist putting on one of her new dresses, and she knew neither Amy nor Chris would be silent about the sudden change in her appearance. But a precariously placed bag of silky, brightly colored underwear convinced her to go in the front door, since the consequences of waiting might be even more embarrassing. With a sigh, she resolved herself to coming reactions.

Juggling her purchases, Eden barely managed to push open the door of her bookstore. The two young women who provided her with such able help turned to greet their customer, then froze in their tracks.

"Eden?" Chris asked.

Her companion was equally stunned. "I don't believe it."

Eden grinned at them. This was better than she expected. She'd never seen either of the girls at a loss for words. She'd known her appearance would amaze them, she thought as Chris and Amy continued to stare at her, openmouthed. In the years they all had worked together, her employees had never seen her in any bright color, much less dazzling red. But this was ridiculous.

Unable to hold the bags any longer, Eden dropped them where she stood and executed a perfect pirouette. "Well? Are you going to say something, Chris?" There was no answer. "Amy?" she inquired of her longtime assistant.

"You . . . uh . . . I . . ." Amy giggled. "I don't know what to say. We've worked together since you bought this place six years ago, and I have never, *ever* seen you in anything so . . . so . . ."

Eden smiled at her lack of words. The red-and-white-print sundress she wore had knocked her eyes out when she'd first seen it. It was pretty and feminine and sexy all at the same time. Just the thing to give a woman confidence. And, as she'd admitted to herself earlier, when dealing with Gabriel, she needed all she could get. He always seemed so at ease, so sure of himself, as if he had no doubt at all that she would agree to whatever he planned, including bed. And last night, first in her apartment, then at dinner, she'd found herself falling under that spell. The only problem was, she had plans of her own. Plans she'd be hard put to carry out if she let herself become infatuated with Gabriel Phillips!

She glanced back at Amy who was still trying to put her ideas into words. "So beautiful?" Eden said helpfully, striking a sultry pose. "So sexy?"

Amy and Chris laughed. "So bright!" they said simultaneously.

Eden laughed along with them. It seemed strange to think it at twenty-eight, but suddenly she felt young again. She bent to pick up a couple of bags. "Wait till you see what else I got!"

Both girls moved forward eagerly. Finally able to find their tongues, they proceeded to exclaim over Eden's new clothes, in between grilling her on the reason for her sudden transformation. A half hour later, the interrogation ended when the telephone rang.

With a groan, Chris went to answer it. "The Book Tree," she said cheerily. "Yes, just a moment, sir." She held out the phone to Eden. "Tell me, boss, does your wonderful metamorphosis have anything to do with the man with the warm, seductive voice at the other end of this line?'' she asked archly.

Eden blushed. It had to be Gabriel. She grinned at the open curiosity on her companions' faces. ''Of course not,'' she said before picking up the receiver, not feeling in the least guilty for her blatant lie.

''This is Eden.''

''Hi, beautiful.'' Gabriel's voice came through, as rich and thick as hot chocolate with marshmallows.

Eden grinned at the thought. If he kept this up, she was going to gain ten pounds! ''Hi, Gabriel,'' she answered, trying to ignore the whispered speculation in which Amy and Chris were engaged.

''I hope you're calling to set up that appointment we talked about.'' She wanted to make it clear to her co-workers that this was a business call. She didn't think she was ready to have Amy and Chris decide she'd suddenly acquired a love life. She'd just met the man, and Lord knew he had an ulterior motive for seeing her.

Realizing Gabriel hadn't answered, Eden scowled. ''Is something wrong?''

''Everything's wrong,'' he said.

He sounded vaguely frantic, and Eden's stomach dropped. ''Is my grandfather all right?'' she asked, unable to keep the fear out of her voice. It would be too awful if something had happened to Matt when she was so close to making peace with him. When Gabriel didn't answer her question, Eden's hands began to shake. ''Gabriel?''

"What? Oh, sorry, Eden, I was talking to my secretary. Things have gone crazy here. It turns out my father had gotten more lax than I thought. Crisis after crisis has been dumped in my lap. And I can't go to him, because his doctor has forbidden it."

Relief flowed through Eden. Thank heavens it wasn't her grandfather, after all.

"I'm afraid we'll have to put off our meeting for a few days."

Once again, butterflies entered Eden's stomach. A delay in their meeting to discuss her book meant a delay in publishing it. And a delay in seeing her grandfather.

Suddenly she wished she hadn't made this stupid plan. She should just go see Matt, face the music. So what if he ridiculed her chosen profession? In a few months, she could hand him *Serena's Lullaby* and show him she wasn't the worthless dreamer he thought.

Oh, yes, Eden, that's the way to think. If she met her grandfather with that attitude, they'd be estranged again in seconds. It was clear she wasn't ready.

"I'm sorry, Eden."

Eden started, forgetting for a moment that Gabriel couldn't read her thoughts. It was a good thing he couldn't, or he'd never stop trying to convince her to see Matt. "It's okay, Gabriel, I understand." What else could she say?

"I'll call you in a few days," he said abstractly and hung up before she could answer.

* * *

A week later Eden entered the Book Tree with a hopeful heart. Surely today she would hear from Gabriel. She didn't know how much longer she could live in this limbo, even if it was of her own creation. The last few nights she'd been having nightmares about her grandfather, dreaming that she couldn't reach him, dreaming that he'd rejected her again. The dreams only convinced her she couldn't agree to see him until the book was done.

Catching sight of Amy, she walked to the counter. "Any calls while I was gone, Amy?" she asked, searching the desk for any telltale messages.

"Not a one, sorry."

Eden shrugged at Amy's sympathetic expression. She'd tried hard not to let her growing dejection show over the last few days. But after six years Amy knew her well enough to see beneath the facade.

Eden took off her damp trench coat and hung it on the old-fashioned oak hat rack.

"Ice cream didn't work, huh?" Amy asked in a disgustingly cheerful voice.

In spite of their sympathy for their boss, neither Amy nor Chris had been able to hide their obvious amusement at her predicament. In spite of her efforts, they wouldn't give up the notion that she and Gabriel were an item. Eden having what they considered a love life—no matter how she protested—was a novelty, and they were exceedingly curious about the man with the sexy voice.

Eden wrinkled her nose at Amy's question. "It might have worked," she said, "but two seconds after I found a nice secluded bench to sit on, it started raining." She picked up a pile of orders she had to make calls on. It was no use putting them off any longer. Gabriel wasn't going to call. "Let me tell you . . ." she added as she walked toward the back office. "Rainstorms and mocha almond fudge do not mix!"

The clock on the mantel tolled midnight as the third victim was strangled in the mystery novel Eden read. She hadn't been able to sleep, and she hadn't been able to write. So she'd curled up on the sofa and picked up a book. Murder and mayhem fit her mood.

Now the fourth victim was being stalked. The murderer carried a sharp, shiny stiletto. He crept up behind the young woman and . . . The phone rang, causing Eden to jump.

Laughing at herself, Eden picked up the receiver. "Hello?"

"Are you in bed?"

Eden's eyes widened. The voice was low and sensuous and excitingly familiar. No wonder Amy and Chris hadn't believed her when she reacted to a simple question like this! "Gabriel?"

"That's promising," he replied, a tinge of humor in his voice.

"What is?"

"You recognized my voice."

Eden laughed, but refrained from telling him she would have known his voice anywhere. She heard it in her dreams. Almost inevitably her nightmares about her grandfather were preceded by some extremely sensual dreams about Gabriel.

"You never answered my question, Eden."

Eden smiled. "No, I'm not in bed. I'm sitting on the couch reading a murder mystery. When the phone rang, it scared me half to death."

He laughed. "Sorry about that."

Eden wasn't in the least sorry. She was just glad he'd called. "Are your crises over?"

"I just solved the last one and wanted to call before I went home."

"You're still at the office?" She suddenly realized he sounded tired and had the urge to comfort him. How had he come to mean so much to her after so brief an acquaintance? She must be nuts to have let him get under her skin like this. She knew as well as he did that it was her grandfather Gabriel wanted her for, not himself. Or was it?

"Yes. I wanted to call and make an appointment for tomorrow afternoon. I'm anxious to get started on *Serena's Lullaby* and I know you are, too."

She was, Eden thought, and for more than one reason. Once the book was published and she met with her grandfather, she would be able to discover once and for all whether Gabriel's seeming attraction for her was real, or manufactured for the purpose of persuading her to see her grandfather.

"What time do you want me to come in tomorrow?"

She heard Gabriel trying to stifle a yawn and smiled.

"Is one o'clock okay?" he asked sleepily. "After our meeting, I'll take you to lunch."

Trying to soften me up? she asked silently. Oh, well, what did it matter? Besides, once he had a chance to know her better, maybe he wouldn't push her so much.

"That sounds fine. I'll see you tomorrow," she said, regretting that she had to be so suspicious. It would have been nice if she could relax enough to enjoy Gabriel's charm without worrying about the reason for it.

"Good night, Eden."

The deep, gentle timbre of his voice enveloped her like a caress. She'd never be able to return to her murder mystery now! "Good night, Gabriel."

Eden hung up the phone feeling tingly and mixed up and more determined than ever. The book *would* get published. She and her grandfather *would* make peace. As for her and Gabriel? "Who knows?" she said aloud and laughing a little as she went off to bed.

An hour before she was to meet Gabriel, Eden took down the painting that hung over her bed. Among other things, her grandmother, Serena, had been a wonderful painter. It had been her thirteenth birthday present from her grandmother and one of the few things Eden had taken with her when she'd left. She remembered being afraid at the time that carrying the huge picture around would make her too memorable to strangers, making it easier for her grandfather to find her. But she couldn't have left without it. It was like taking her grandmother with her.

Eden placed the framed canvas on the length of butcher paper in which she planned to wrap it for the trip downtown. The scene her grandmother had re-created was the Connecticut River Valley at dawn in early summer. The sun was just beginning to sparkle off the morning mist. The hills and trees still held a hint of spring green. The river seemed to flow along lazily. The aura of the painting spoke of peace, beauty, and serenity, everything that was Serena. It would be a perfect illustration for the dust jacket of the book.

Eden wrapped and taped the painting, then took one more look in the mirror. "You're not going anywhere dressed like that, young lady! Cover yourself right now," a voice demanded. It was her grandfather's, once again showing how much he disapproved of her. "No granddaughter of mine is showing herself in public looking like a tart."

Tears filled the grown-up Eden's eyes, just as they had the teenager's. She hadn't dressed any differently from the other girls at school, but because she'd filled out her clothes better, her grandfather had assumed she was a tramp.

He would have hated the bright pink lipstick she wore. The mascara and blusher would have made him furious. Eden turned away from the mirror and walked to the bed. Wearing her new clothes hadn't bothered her all week. Why did it have to start now? She looked at the cool comforter and soft pillows longingly. What she wanted more than anything right now was to throw herself on the bed and have a good cry, but she couldn't afford the time. She had an appointment.

For a brief moment she considered changing her clothes, but then she raised her head with pride. She wasn't a teenager anymore. Her grandfather had no control over what she did or what she wore. She'd be damned if . . . A thought occurred to her. What if Gabriel thought she was doing this for him? He'd think he was getting to her and would probably turn up the heat. God, that was all she needed! Her body already reacted to him as if he was a flower and she was a bee.

No! She couldn't take the chance. She kicked off her new pumps and began to undress. It didn't matter that the skirt and blouse she wore were perfectly respectable. Suddenly the bright colors of her new clothes seemed so obvious, as if she was saying, "Take me, I'm yours." The frilly lingerie she wore underneath seemed to prove that was what she wanted.

Eden turned abruptly and walked to the bathroom, where she washed off her makeup. The cool water didn't help. Her cheeks were still rosy from her emotions, her eyes still bright. Well, there was nothing she could do. She went back into the bedroom.

Eden pulled a brown corduroy skirt and print blouse out of the closet. Back to the old Eden, she thought. The point of this meeting was to get her book published, not to seduce Gabriel Phillips.

Gabriel glanced up as Eden walked into the room and sighed inwardly. How had they gone back to square one? he thought. After their dinner together, he'd thought Eden had relaxed. Their phone conversation last night hadn't given the slightest hint of the hostility that flashed from her gray eyes. He'd even allowed himself to hope that the delay in this meeting would cause no problems.

He'd been wrong. She'd clearly retreated into her shell, and he suspected he'd have a harder time than ever trying to convince her to see her grandfather.

Finally noticing the unwieldy package Eden had maneuvered through the door, Gabriel moved around the desk to take it from her. "Here, let me help."

Eden smiled, surprising him. "Thank you."

For what seemed an eternity, Gabriel's gaze refused to release itself from the charm of that smile. Not for the first time he wondered what had driven this lovely young woman to a life of drabness and seclusion. What was wrong with men these days?

"Please sit down." He motioned to a comfortable armchair which sat in front of his desk. He had been planning on returning to his own chair behind the desk, but as Eden sat, he caught a tantalizing glimpse of lace through the opening of her blouse. The sight intrigued him; a week ago he would have bet she was into plain cotton. Maybe she wasn't wrapped as tightly as he thought.

Gabriel perched on the edge of the desk and smiled. "I'm glad we could finally get together. I'm sorry about the delay, but things around here were a mess."

"I understand," Eden said. "Everything fine now?"

"Yes, and we can go full speed ahead on your book."

Eden let out a small sigh of relief that surprised him. He knew the book was important, but surely a small delay couldn't matter that much. Was that the reason for the hostility?

"Can you give me an idea how long it will take to release the book?"

Her tone was cool, as if the answer didn't matter one way or another, and it confused Gabriel. One minute she was acting relieved that they were finally going to publish her book, the next she was acting like she didn't give a damn.

"Months—between designing, editing, printing, and finding an illustrator for the cover."

Eden jumped up and started unwrapping the package. "The cover illustration's no problem. I have it right here."

She stood back to reveal the most beautiful painting Gabriel had ever seen. He gazed at Eden. "This is one of Serena's, isn't it?" he asked, remembering several works scattered around Matt's home.

Eden didn't take her eyes from the picture. "She gave it to me on my thirteenth birthday."

A world of pain seemed to underlie Eden's simple words, but Gabriel decided not to pry. One wrong word and he had a feeling Eden would go running out the door. "You're right about it being perfect for the cover. I'm glad you brought it."

Eden smiled. "I hope this will speed up the process."

Gabriel frowned a little, wondering at her need to rush. "Well, it will, some. But even with the painting, it will still be at least four months before the first book comes off the presses."

"Four months? *Four months?*" She dropped into her chair. How could she put off her grandfather that long? She glanced at Gabriel who seemed to have found something fascinating just around her top button. How could she put off Gabriel?

Eden stood slowly to face him. "No! That's totally unacceptable."

SEVEN

Gabriel's gaze leapt to Eden's face. "I beg your pardon?"

Eden returned his stare. "You heard me. Four months is much too long. You have to put the book out sooner."

Gabriel couldn't believe his ears. "Sooner? Four months is at the least. It could take longer. *Serena's Lullaby* isn't some rinky-dink paperback. It's going to take time and care to . . ."

"Rinky-dink? Is that what you think of my other books?"

Eden's tone was outraged, and Gabriel didn't blame her. Rinky-dink had been his father's favorite term for the books Gabriel helped publish whenever he wanted his son to feel guilty for leaving the family firm.

"No, it isn't. Your historicals are wonderful. I'm just trying to explain that we can't just whip out *Serena's Lullaby* as if it were so much—"

"Trash?" Eden asked pleasantly, but the look in her eyes belied her voice.

"No, not trash!" Gabriel said defensively. In his entire thirty-five years he had never had such a hard time choosing words as he was having right now. "Besides, we do have other books to publish, you know."

Eden eased down into the chair, crossing her legs in a movement Gabriel thought was unconsciously sensual . . . until she looked up at him through her thick lashes. "Yes, but none of the others are going to bring as large an audience as mine will."

Gabriel stared at her. Where had the arrogance come from? What happened to the shy, demure woman he'd been dealing with? Maybe she was just being candid. After all, what she said was true. But her expression seemed to say more than that. It was as if she held a trump card.

The phone rang behind him, making him jump. Grateful for the interruption, Gabriel moved to answer it.

"Phillips."

Matt Pendleton's familiar voice greeted him. "Hi, Matt. What's up?" He glanced over at Eden, but her face was turned away from him.

Suddenly a thought occurred to him so he barely heard Matt's answer, although he knew it had something to do with his father. Jerrod Phillips often called Matt to pump him for information about Gabriel's handling of the firm, even though Jerrod's doctors had expressly forbidden him to have anything to do with business.

"Don't worry about it," Gabriel told his old friend. "I'll call Dad and take care of it." Whatever *it* was, he thought. At that moment, he didn't care. He was too busy planning his own trump card.

Gabriel hung up the phone and studied Eden, who was studiously trying to ignore him. It was clear to him that she was more interested in her grandfather than she liked to let on.

"You really want this book out in a hurry, don't you?"

Eden looked up and shrugged. "I'm like this with all my books. Once I'm finished, I can't wait to see them in print."

Gabriel didn't believe that for a minute. She had some other reason for her need to rush. Unfortunately, he had no idea what that reason was. "I'll tell you what," he said, waiting until he had her full attention before continuing. "I'll cut the publishing time of your book in half, on one condition."

Eden's expression became wary, not unexpectedly. "What condition?"

"That you call your grandfather immediately and let him know where, and how, you are."

Eden looked down at her hands. The longer she was silent, the stronger Gabriel's hopes grew. If getting the book out was that important to her, she'd have to agree. He suspected that deep down she really wanted to see her grandfather. This would give her the perfect excuse. Maybe it was just what she needed, someone to make the decision for her.

Eden brought her head up, and Gabriel held his breath. "All right, Gabriel, you win . . ." She stood and picked up her purse.

Gabriel smiled. *This is great,* he thought. *Matt will finally have his granddaughter back, and I'll finally have a chance to get to know Eden with no barriers between us.*

His elation faded as he realized Eden had walked to the door. He stared at her in confusion. "Where are you going?"

The expression in her eyes was cold as ice. "Home. I guess four months is acceptable after all." She opened the door and walked out, slamming it behind her.

The bang of the door was all she needed to start her tears flowing. Eden wiped at them furiously. Damn Gabriel Phillips! How could he do that to her?

She walked across the hall and punched the button for the elevator. The doors opened immediately, and she stepped in. Alone in the empty space, Eden let out a sigh. Why was it always so easy to forget that it was her grandfather whom Gabriel cared about? Sure, he looked at her sometimes as if she was a tall glass of water and he was dying of thirst. But obviously any attraction he had for her was physical. And considering the way she dressed, even that could be false, a mere ruse to lull her into trusting him enough to do what he wanted.

Remembering the fire in his gaze, Eden didn't think so, though. Everything about this man gave off the aura of heat lightning during a summer storm, leaving her feeling as buffeted as a single stalk of wheat. That kind of sexual connection couldn't be faked, could it? Oh, well, it didn't matter. Until the book was out and she'd seen her grandfather, she couldn't act on her attraction for Gabriel, either.

Eden half smiled. It was almost funny when she thought about it. He was willing to move up the publication date on her book in order to get her to see her grandfather. And she wanted the publication date moved up so she could take it to her grandfather sooner. Basically, they both wanted the same thing.

At the ground floor, the elevator doors slid open to reveal a slightly winded Gabriel. He stepped in front of Eden, preventing her from exiting. Keeping one hand on her arm, he reached back to push the button for his floor.

"What do you think you're doing?" Eden protested, trying to pull her arm away.

Gabriel's hold remained firm. "What do you think *you're* doing? Why did you run out?"

Eden flung her head back. "Why should I have stayed? You made your position perfectly clear. The only way you'll bring up the publication date is if I call my grandfather. Since I have no intention of doing that right now, I guess we're back to the original time frame.''

Gabriel removed his hand from her arm, his eyes narrowed. "You're really something, Eden Pendleton. You always have to be in control, don't you?''

Genuinely surprised at his comment, Eden gazed at him. "What are you talking about?''

His hands resting on his hips, Gabriel shook his head in disbelief. "What am I talking about? I'll tell you what I'm talking about. This!'' He flicked his hand toward her. "When I first met you, I thought these drab things you wear meant you'd been hurt. I thought they were a means of protection. Now I realize they're just a means of control. You aren't going to go out of your way to attract a man. Just like you aren't going to go out of your way to get in touch with your grandfather.''

Eden looked away from the anger in Gabriel's green eyes. "You don't know what you're talking about.'' she muttered.

The doors of the elevator opened, and Gabriel pulled Eden across the hall to his office. Eden tried to yank her wrist from his hand, but even though she felt no pain, Gabriel's grip was unyielding. "Gabriel, let me go!'' she ordered.

"No!'' He slammed the door behind them, making Eden's stomach drop to her feet.

"I know exactly what I'm talking about. I can't tell Matt I've found you, because I won't hurt him by telling him you refuse to see him. You *are* in control of that. But you won't be in control of me, lady!'' He pulled her to him.

Eden looked up in surprise. ''What are you doing?''

Gabriel's half smile both frightened and excited Eden. She willed her body not to react to his nearness, but it did no good. ''Gabriel . . .''

''Shut up!'' Gabriel whispered against her lips.

Any protest she might have made was lost in the searing sensation of Gabriel's kiss. His mouth felt hot and dry against hers, like an Indian summer's day that threatens to melt your bones. A raging thirst grew within her, a thirst quickly satisfied as his moist tongue tangled with her own.

No resistance came to the surface, only relief. This might have started out as a way of his taking control, but it had turned into a gift of passion. Joy filled her as she accepted his offering, taking it greedily, yet giving her own in return. To Eden, they seemed as one, their hearts pounding in the same rhythm, their souls beating with life. Gabriel Phillips was the most compelling, attractive man she'd ever met, and to have to put him off for months was more than she could bear.

Gabriel lifted his head, leaving Eden feeling bereft. She had wanted the kiss to go on forever. Reluctantly, she opened her eyes to look at the man who had made her feel so much. He was smiling slightly, but as if *be*mused, not *a*mused, and Eden knew he was as affected as she. She gazed into his eyes, unable to pull herself from the flames that seemed to draw her in, like the heat that draws the fog from the sea.

Gabriel reached up a hand to cup the side of her face. "It seems I don't have as much control over this situation as I thought."

Eden barely managed a smile, for the touch of his hand was having almost as much of an effect as his kiss.

Gabriel's expression became serious. "I can't let you walk out, Eden. We can work out whatever disagreements we have about your book. And I'll help you handle whatever problems you have with your grandfather. But I can't let you go!"

Elation filled up every pore of her body. Gabriel really wanted her to stay. "Gabriel . . ."

"Look, I don't know what happened to you in the past. I think you need to control everything because you're afraid of being hurt, and I have no intention of doing that. I want very much for you to reconcile with Matt, but I didn't kiss you for your grandfather. I kissed you for *me*."

Eden wanted to throw herself into Gabriel's arms. It would have been so easy to give herself up to his strength, to let him act as a liaison with her grandfather. But she couldn't. She'd made her plans, and she had to go through with them.

Eden stepped back from him. "This is moving much too fast for me. I hardly know you." Heavens, she sounded like she was some virginal twenty-year-old from the forties. "Look, I'm not trying to be coy. But it's true. We've only seen each other a few times."

Gabriel moved closer. "Don't deny what you felt with me, Eden."

"I'm not trying to deny it."

"Then what *are* you trying to do?" he asked gently.

Oh, hell, Eden thought. How should she know what she was trying to do? The lemony scent of his cologne had invaded her senses, making it almost impossible to answer his question. "I think I'm trying to suggest that we get to know each other better."

Gabriel smiled. "Are you asking me out on a date?"

Eden blushed. "Don't tease. I'm just . . . uh . . ."

His grin widened. "Uh?"

Oh, well, there was no use denying it. "All right, yes, I *am* asking you out on a date."

When Gabriel just stood there smiling, Eden began to get nervous. "Well?"

Gabriel clapped his hands together. "I think it's a great idea! We'll start with lunch."

"Lunch?"

"Sure, there's this charming little bed and breakfast place just down the street."

Eden couldn't help but grin at his teasing. "I don't think that would be appropriate."

"Then I guess it'll have to be the seafood place down on the wharf. You do like fish, don't you?"

"I love it," she said aloud. But in her head, another phrase was going round and round. *I love you*, it said. And no matter how she tried, it just wouldn't go away.

By the time Gabriel arrived home that evening, he was feeling so terrific he almost skipped up the walkway. Lunch with Eden had gone great. Not only had she become more relaxed with him, especially after he'd agreed to push up the publication date, but he had been happy to learn that Eden's vision of the book matched his own. It would be a wonderful tribute to Serena Pendleton. The one dark spot of the whole day, he thought as he slipped the key into the lock, was that he couldn't tell Matt about the book.

Oh, well, someday soon. He was sure once Eden got to know *him* better, she would begin to trust his opinion of her grandfather and would decide to see him. The best part was they could start tomorrow night, since she had agreed to have dinner with him.

"Gabe, is that you?" Matt came into the hallway looking vaguely distressed. "Did you call Jerrod? He's been driving me nuts. I keep telling him I don't know anything about the business, but he won't let up."

Gabriel smiled at his old friend. Even the thought of his irascible father wasn't going to ease his good mood today. "Don't worry about Dad. I'll take care of him."

He studied Matt's face. In spite of his illness and depression, he was still a handsome, distinguished-looking man. Tall, straight, and slender, it was clear Eden had inherited her lithe build from him.

"Don't worry, he says," Matt muttered as he walked back through the living room with its gorgeous view of the city below. "It's getting where I'm afraid to answer the phone."

Following him into the kitchen, Gabriel laughed. "I'm sure it's not that bad. You and Dad have a lot in common."

"Huh!" was Matt's only answer as he began to set the table.

"I'm sorry Dad gave you such a bad time," Gabriel said sincerely, although he half suspected Matt enjoyed every minute of his wrangling with Jerrod Phillips. "How was your day besides that? Are you feeling okay?"

"I'm fine! Quit asking me that all the time. You fuss at me like a mother hen. That's one thing I can say for Jerrod. He never asks me how I'm feeling. Sit down. Mrs. Ames left lasagna for dinner tonight."

"Sounds great." Gabriel sat at the table. It had been a while since he'd dared to help Matt with dinner preparations. He was too fond of his ears to lose them. For a moment, he couldn't help wondering if it was Matt's irascibility that had scared off Eden.

He couldn't imagine it of today's Eden, but maybe at eighteen she had been a lot meeker.

". . . Connecticut."

Gabriel brought his attention back to Matt who set a steaming plate of lasagna in front of him. "What about Connecticut?" he asked after realizing he'd missed something.

"I said, I'm thinking about going back home."

Gabriel's fork landed with a clatter on his plate. "You can't!"

Matt sat down across from him. "What do you mean I can't? I can do anything I want."

Gabriel's stomach churned as he tried to come up with a valid excuse for keeping Matt here. Damn Eden for being so stubborn, he thought.

He took a deep breath. "I'm just saying you're not well enough to live on your own yet."

"That's ridiculous! I'm perfectly fine."

"You are not perfectly fine!"

Matt shook his head. "All right, maybe not perfectly. But good enough to go home. I do have people around if I need help."

"Right! A housekeeper and a gardener/handyman who are nearly the same age as you." Gabriel leaned back in his chair trying to think quickly. Why did this have to happen now?

"Bunk! The Rizzis are healthy as horses and entirely capable of taking care of me. *If* I needed taking care of, which I don't!" he concluded, pounding his fist against the table.

"Well, I do!"

Matt regarded him skeptically, but Gabriel decided to take his shot. "You know how hard I've been working. Now you're planning on leaving me to come home to an empty house and no dinner."

"Ha! I don't make the dinners. Mrs. Ames does. All I do is heat them up. Something I'm sure you can handle. Now, eat your food before I have to heat it up again." He picked up his fork and dug into his lasagna.

Gabriel watched Matt eat with relish. He really had gotten better. There was barely a sign of his stroke left. Gabriel saw a barely perceptible expression of sadness flit over Matt's face. There was something else going on here.

"What's the real reason you want to go back East, Matt?"

"I told you the reason," Matt said grumpily.

"Maybe part of it, but there's something else, isn't there?"

Matt put his fork down and looked at Gabriel. "It's Eden."

Gabriel's breath caught. "Eden?"

Matt nodded. "I was a fool to think we could find her, that she'd want to come back. I'm not a young man, but I've still got some life left. Maybe it's time I got back to that life and quit wasting time on futile hopes."

More than anything Gabriel wanted to tell Matt he'd found Eden. But he'd be damned if he'd raise his friend's hopes only to crush them again. Eden refused to see him now. But he knew she'd agree soon. She had to. All he needed was a little more time.

"See, you aren't saying a word. You think it's hopeless, too, don't you?" Matt asked, his expression still asking for reassurance.

Gabriel took a deep breath. "No, I don't. I . . . uh, didn't want to tell you this."

Matt leaned forward. "Tell me what? Do you have a lead?"

Resigned to his lie, Gabriel nodded. "Yes, I talked to someone the other day who's sure he met her here on the West Coast."

"Where on the West Coast?" Matt asked eagerly.

Gabriel's brain was working a mile a minute trying to come up with something that would buy him time. "That's just it, he doesn't know. This guy I talked to . . . for the last five years he's traveled from San Diego to British Columbia for his company. So he's not sure where he met her. He's going to look up some old files when he gets back to San Francisco. But it might take a while."

Matt half smiled. "Then I guess you have a houseguest for a little longer. It's not much. But at least it's something. And if my Eden's on the West Coast there's no way I'm going back East. How long before this guy gets back to you?

Gabriel couldn't believe his story had worked. He

was sure Matt would see through it. "A couple of weeks, maybe more."

"This might turn out to be a dead end, you know," Matt said kindly.

Gabriel immediately felt guilty. Matt was trying to comfort *him*! "I don't think it will. I have a feeling you're going to be seeing your granddaughter sooner than you think." *If I don't strangle said granddaughter first for what she's putting both of us through!* Gabriel thought vehemently.

EIGHT

Was she *nuts*? Eden thought as she hung up the phone. Had she really agreed to take the day off to drive over to the coast with Gabriel?

Shaking her head, she walked over to the large window that overlooked the street and the small park across the way. It was an hour-and-a-half-trip to Oceanside. Add to that a meal and whatever else he had planned and they were looking to spend at least six hours together. How the heck was she supposed to handle being alone with Gabriel for six hours?

A flock of birds lifting from a small pond in the park caught her eye. It was a beautiful day, she thought. Now that the latest storm had blown away it would probably be gorgeous on the coast. As for work, it wasn't as if Amy and Chris couldn't handle the shop by themselves. They did it often when she was working on a book. But *six hours* alone in a car with Gabriel?

She turned from the window. Gabriel had said he had a couple of things to do at the office. She could call him and cancel. She walked over to the phone and reached for the receiver, then let her hand fall to her side. There was one little problem. She *wanted* to go.

Actually, there was another problem, she thought as she walked to her bedroom. What was she going to wear? She threw open the doors of the closet. Hanging next to her usual drab clothes were the new clothes she had bought. Their very brightness made the old ones look even worse.

She took out a pair of designer jeans and a soft pink sweater and laid them on the bed. In a way the original dinner out would have been easier not only for her to dress for, but because a ride to the coast left them with too much time to talk. She took off the gray sweats she wore and put on the new outfit.

A restaurant would have been far less intimate, she thought as she studied herself in the mirror. The very idea of that intimacy gave her an urge to protect herself, to don some kind of shell. And this outfit wasn't going to do it. She pulled off the form-fitting sweater and stepped out of the slim jeans.

Tearing a pair of brown cords and an old sweater from the closet, she put them on. *Good! these feel much better,* she thought, until she looked in the mirror. She groaned aloud. "I can't wear this outfit. It looks terrible." She dropped on the bed and covered her face with her hands. Now what?

She lay back and stared up at the ceiling, feeling as if she sat on a rickety old fence. On one side was a muddy bog, on the other, bubbling quicksand. If she suddenly turned up in those tight jeans and the fitted pink sweater, Gabriel would think she was dressing up for him. And although that might be partly true, it might be more telling if she dressed as usual, sort of as a test to see if he was interested in her or in her connection to her grandfather.

Eden sat up. Playing this kind of game was dangerous. There was no way she could really know the answer. He could be going out with her dressed as she was because he wanted her to see her grandfather, or he could really be interested in *her* and not care how she dressed.

"Well, I know one thing," she said, standing, "I can't stand wearing these." She took off her cords and pulled on her jeans. "I'm a woman. What normal woman could have a closet full of new clothes and not wear any of them?"

Looking at the result in the mirror, she decided her oversize sweater looked almost stylish with slim-legged jeans. But it needed color, she thought, searching through the closet.

Gabriel took the steps to Eden's apartment two at a time. It had pleased and surprised him when she had agreed to this drive. He smiled. Maybe she was beginning to trust him after all. He rapped on the door.

A few moments later, Eden opened the door. Gabriel glanced from the nervous smile on her lips to the long braid that fell across her shoulder to her outfit, which he suspected was the reason for her uneasiness. Without saying anything, she seemed to be asking for his approval. He smiled, feeling touched by the need she tried so hard to hide. "You look great," he said.

She motioned him in. "Thanks," she said briefly. "I'll get my jacket."

He could almost see her withdraw into her shell and was sadly amused. She had no reason to retreat. What he'd said was true. Although she looked like a young girl who'd confiscated one of her big brother's sweaters, the result was endearing, making the tall, buxom Eden look delicate and fragile. Threads of orange, gold, and blue highlighted the mixed browns of the sweaters. The orange cotton turtleneck she wore underneath brought out a brightness in her gray eyes, and the slim fit of the jeans made her legs look a mile long.

Eden came out of the bedroom wearing a gray quilted down coat. "I'm ready when you are."

Gabriel opened the front door, hiding his grin. She sounded as if they were going to an execution instead of a nice drive in the country.

*   *   *

In the car, Eden took a deep breath and tried to relax. She shouldn't have come. *He hasn't started the car yet,* she told herself. *Tell him you've changed your mind. Go ahead, tell him!* But the words wouldn't come.

Gabriel turned on the ignition and the car started forward, leaving her chance behind.

A half hour later, entering the Forest Grove city limits, Eden wondered if Gabriel thought she'd left her voice behind, too. He'd kept up a steady stream of small talk, but she'd only answered yes or no. She'd never been so nervous with a man in her life!

Eden's head jerked up as Gabriel pulled the car over to the curb. She looked around. "This is Pacific University. Why have we stopped here?"

He turned in his seat, so he faced her. His expression was serious, his green eyes questioning. "Is something wrong?"

She looked down at her hands, damp from her nervousness, then out at the tree-covered campus. "No, of course not."

"If I explode that time bomb you seem to be waiting for, will it make you feel better?"

She turned her head to stare at him. "What?"

"Aren't you waiting for me to ask you to go see Matt?"

Eden almost laughed. She'd been so caught up in her feelings about Gabriel she hadn't given a thought to her grandfather. She studied his face closely. "Is that why you asked me to go on a long drive with you? Make me a captive audience, so to speak."

He smiled. "If that's what you thought, why did you agree to come with me?"

For the life of her she couldn't come up with an answer, or at least one she wanted to give.

His grin widened. "Shall I answer for you?"

She wished she could tell what he was thinking, but all she saw in his eyes was humor. He made her want to laugh with him. "Go ahead," she said, wanting to know what he'd concocted in that extraordinary mind of his.

He nodded. "You came because you wanted to. No other reason. No ulterior motives."

She looked away from his green eyes which seemed to glow with an inner light. "You sound very sure of yourself."

"I am," he said firmly. "And do you know why?"

She shook her head, then felt his fingers on her chin, gently turning her so she had to look at him. His big, warm hand cupped her face, causing myriad sensations, all of which made her want to kiss his palm.

"I know," he said, gazing into her eyes, "because I wanted to be with you. No other reason."

She smiled. "No ulterior motives?"

He shook his head. "Not a one."

She closed her eyes briefly and moved back from his hand. Maybe she could handle hours with

Gabriel, but if he kept touching her like that, she couldn't guarantee that she wouldn't throw herself into his arms. And once he knew how she really felt, she didn't have a chance of keeping him at arm's length until she was ready to see her grandfather.

She looked over at Gabriel, who sat staring out the window. She might have to stay out of his arms, but she had no intention of depriving herself of his company. "So, what are we waiting for?" she asked.

Gabriel's gaze came back to her. He looked as if his thoughts had been far away. "What?"

She allowed herself a teasing smile. "Are we going to the coast or not?"

Without a word, he started the motor, pulled into traffic, and headed west.

"I think I could drive this road blindfolded," Eden said after they'd been driving a while. "I take this trip whenever I'm having trouble with a book. For some reason, it's easier to think when I'm driving."

Gabriel smiled, happy to hear her sounding so relaxed. "I know what you mean."

Eden laughed, surprising him. He didn't think he'd ever heard her laugh before. "What's so funny?"

She laid her head against the headrest. "I was just remembering. One day I got so involved in trying to solve a plot problem that time just went out of my head. The next thing I knew I saw a sign for the Oregon Dunes."

He glanced at her, laughing. "That's two hundred miles from Portland!"

She nodded. "I know. It took me almost four hours to get home . . . Oh, look, there's the ocean."

Gabriel pulled the car off the road and turned off the motor.

"Isn't it beautiful?" Eden asked, gazing out at the gray-green waves pounding against the rocks.

"Beautiful," Gabriel said, but he wasn't looking at the sea. He had expected this drive to make things easier. If he had a chance to get to know Eden, he knew he could come up with a way to convince her to see Matt. Now he wasn't so sure getting to know her better was the best approach.

When he'd first met her, his masculinity had been challenged by her refusal to show her femininity. Maybe he'd seen *My Fair Lady* too many times, but he'd had the urge to transform her into his idea of what a woman should look like. When he'd seen her accomplish her own transformation in the park, he'd been intrigued by the beautiful woman beneath the drab shell.

Eden opened her door and stepped out. "Let's go walk on the beach," she said, not waiting for him to follow.

Gabriel climbed out of the car and watched her run lithely down the slope. What had begun as a physical attraction had turned into something more. He'd felt it earlier when he'd touched her cheek and gazed into her eyes.

"Come on, Gabriel!" she called. "This is terrific!"

Gabriel slid down the slope, never taking his eyes from the charming nymph who laughed with the wind. There was no denying that he wanted her, but he cared about her, too. And that was what scared him, because it was those feelings, he suspected, that would complicate things way beyond his control. *I sure hope you know what you're doing,* he told himself as he ran to catch up with Eden.

Feeling the need for fresh air, Gabriel parked his car on the street then walked around the building to the alley that led to Eden's steps. Seeing a soda can, he kicked it aggressively. The last two weeks had done nothing to ease the feelings of foreboding that had materialized that day on the beach. He felt like he was in the middle of a dangerous jungle. One wrong step either way, with Matt or Eden, and he'd be doomed.

Eden had obviously been shopping, because she had been dressing more colorfully and looking more beautiful every time he saw her. But whenever he tried to give her a compliment, she retreated into her shell. To make things worse, Matt had been talking about going home again, and it was taking all Gabriel's a brainpower to come up with reasons for him to stay.

He kicked another can, then thinking he'd better calm his emotions before seeing Eden, he decided to take a walk around the block. So what if he was late. Better that than snapping off Eden's head the moment she opened the door.

Eden glanced at the mantel clock as she ran from her bedroom to the bathroom, hoping that for once Gabriel would be late. She wasn't nearly ready to face him. She'd left the shop early in order to get ready, then spent the afternoon sitting by the window brooding.

This damn test she'd put Gabriel to had been a terrible mistake. She couldn't seem to relax around him. The prettier she dressed, the more he complimented her, the greater her need to withdraw. She couldn't blame Gabriel. He'd responded like any normal man would.

No, it was her. In the end it had occurred to her that there were two ways she could prove to herself that Gabriel cared—number one was to never see her grandfather and see if Gabriel forgave her and stayed with her; number two was to see Matt and find out if once Gabriel's mission was accomplished he would still want her.

It had only taken a moment to decide that she couldn't choose number one. She needed to see her grandfather. She needed to prove herself to him. As for number two, Eden thought as she put the finishing touches on her makeup, that couldn't be accomplished until *Serena's Lullaby* was in print.

She walked back into the bedroom to take a final look in the mirror. This was the first dress she'd worn that was completely new. She was glad she'd let Amy talk her into wearing it. The off-the-shoulder white dress managed to look classy and sexy at the same time. It set off her mother's ruby and diamond pendant to perfection.

The doorbell rang, and her stomach dropped to her feet. She had a feeling this dress would signal a new direction in her and Gabriel's relationship. She wasn't totally sure she was prepared for that change, but knowing it was inevitable, she refused to hide behind the old, drab Eden.

She took a deep, steadying breath, then opened the door. What she saw took her breath away. Always handsome, tonight Gabriel looked magnificent. The dull glow from the porch light brought the red highlights in his hair to flaming life while deepening his green eyes to radiant emerald, putting the same jeweled tone in his silk tie to shame. The fit of his stylish black suit was enhanced by his big, muscular frame, and his shirt was a cool gleaming white next to his warm, tanned skin. From his neatly tamed hair to his newly shined shoes he was the picture of masculine perfection. And she *wanted* him.

"You look beautiful," he said simply, but the look in his eyes was much more complicated.

"Thank you," she answered, finding it strange that this time she didn't feel the least urge to withdraw. Feeling quite terrific, she smiled. "So do you."

He grinned. "Are you sure you want to go *out* to dinner?"

No, I'm not, she thought, weighing the options if they should stay here. Gabriel had been very circumspect the last couple of weeks, and she had appreciated it—all the more because she had seen the heat in his eyes when they'd been close. She thought of the heroines of her books who, more often than not, had thrown caution to the wind and thrown themselves into the arms of the men they loved. Then she looked at Gabriel, whose expression showed marked interest at her delay in answering.

Prudence won out. "I'm sure," she said. The amused skepticism in his eyes told her she didn't sound it. She wrinkled her nose at him. "I'll go get my coat."

Gabriel gazed at Eden across the candlelit table. She seemed so different, relaxed, confident. She hadn't retreated an inch when he'd complimented her. Maybe now was the time to ask about her past. The jungle he'd been living in had become intolerable. He wanted to be free of the restraints that kept him from pursuing a life with Eden. But until they cleared the air between them regarding Matt, he knew there was no chance of them getting together.

"Eden?"

She looked up from her chocolate mousse. "This is terrific." His expression must have been very serious, because her smile faded. "Is something wrong?"

He shook his head, wondering if he dared come right out and ask her what happened between her and Matt. Remembering her earlier reactions to his questioning, he decided he had to come up with a less direct way to broach the subject.

"I was just thinking about my . . . parents." *Right, Gabriel,* he told himself, disgusted at the lame reason he'd invented.

She put her spoon on the small dessert plate. "Your dad's pretty ill, isn't he?"

He was a little surprised that she'd remembered. "Yes . . . no. He'll be okay once he accepts the fact that his publishing company will get by just fine without him."

"It's been hard on you," she said sympathetically.

He might have felt guilty at his unintentional manipulation if she hadn't just given him the opening he needed. "At least I still have my parents. It must have been tough losing your folks at such a young age."

A faraway look came to her eyes as she fingered the strand of pearls at her neck. "It was. Especially since my grandmother had just died a few months before."

"I'm glad you had your grandfather to take care of you."

Her expression hardened. "Did I?"

Gabriel couldn't help but wonder at the change in her. "Didn't Matt become your guardian?"

"Yes, as far as that goes."

What does that mean? he thought, studying Eden's face, which she had turned away from him to stare out the window at the night-darkened Columbia River. A tugboat drifted by, toot-tooting its horn at a passing sailboat.

"Do you hear that whistle?" she asked, not looking at him, her tone soft and distant. "When I was a teenager, I used to lie in bed waiting for the sound of the midnight train rumbling through the darkness. I never knew where it was going, but every single night, at twelve-ten, the whistle would blow, whispering to me of freedom." She turned to him, a determined set to her chin. "And I swore," she said distinctly, "that the first moment I could, I would escape from my grandfather and his coldness."

Gabriel winced at the hurt in her eyes. It, like their color, matched her grandfather's. "But he loved you," he said, not understanding any of this.

She glared at him. "Did he? Then why wasn't he there for me when I was being laughed at and ridiculed? Why didn't he see all my friends disappearing? I needed him so badly, and he abandoned me as surely as if he left me in the gutter!"

Gabriel wanted to cry out at her pain. He wanted to hold her, to comfort her. But an emotionless mask had come down over her face.

"I want to go home," she said. Picking up her

purse, she stood. "I'll meet you in the lobby," she added, then left the dining room.

Gabriel thought he'd never felt so helpless. He signaled the waiter for the check. Her words had confused him, though her pain had been clear. Why had her friends left her? What reason had they had for ridiculing her? And how could the warm, loving man who had helped him through his own grief have turned into the cold, unfeeling man his granddaughter reviled?

He had to know the answers.

NINE

Gabriel didn't know which was more oppressive, the atmosphere outside the car, where the heavy air signaled the coming storm, or the atmosphere inside, where the tension emanating from the silent Eden threatened explosion.

His grip tightened on the steering wheel. Maybe he shouldn't have pushed her. Even her refusal to see Matt hadn't given him an inkling of the depth of hatred she felt for her grandfather. His only hope was that her alienation from him was due as much to her love for him as her hate.

One thing he did know—it was too late to turn back now. He cared about both Matt and Eden, and somehow, he had to come up with a way to get them together. And that meant finding out the answers to the questions that had been rumbling around his brain since Eden's outburst at the restaurant.

He pulled into her alley just as it started to rain. After parking next to her car, he turned off the ignition.

"You don't have to walk me up." Eden's voice was quiet and firm, her dismissal clear.

"Oh, yes, I do," Gabriel returned with equal firmness. He might empathize with her transparent desire to escape, but this time he had no intention of letting her get away without an explanation.

"Gabriel . . ."

"Stay there, I'll come around and get you. I have an umbrella in the trunk."

While retrieving the umbrella, he wondered how he was going to find out what he wanted to know. If she didn't want to talk, he couldn't force her. Maybe if he phrased his questions just right . . .

He opened her door and held out his hand. Silently Eden refused to take it. He wasn't surprised. Her face was so pale she looked like a piece of fragile porcelain that one touch could shatter. He followed her up to the landing, taking the key from her when she couldn't fit it into the lock. He pushed open the door and motioned her in.

She took a step, flipped a light switch, then turned, holding her hand out for the keys. "Good-bye. Thank you for dinner."

Gabriel had to smile. "Nice try, Eden, but I'm

not leaving. We have to talk." He closed the door behind him.

She pulled her coat tighter around her, as if she were freezing, then walked over to the fireplace and started crumpling paper. "Why don't we just drop it? You and I see my grandfather in two different ways," she said as she added kindling to the paper. "Can't we just agree to disagree?"

He watched her strike a match and light the paper. "I don't expect you to agree with me. But I do want to know why you feel the way you do."

After placing two good-size logs on the burning pile, she brushed off her hands and turned to him, a stubborn look on her face. "It's none of your business."

He looked her straight in the eye. "Everything about you is my business," he said, not even trying to keep the seductive edge out of his voice.

A sheen a tears covered her eyes before she turned away.

Gabriel sighed. "Okay, Eden. If you don't want to talk about your grandfather, tell me about those friends of yours. Why did they ridicule you?"

She jerked around, tore off her coat and threw it on a chair. "Do you like the way I look, Gabriel?"

He didn't bother giving her an answer she already knew.

She half smiled. "Yes . . . well, so did the boys."

"The boys?"

"The boys in high school. Except for a few minor

changes, *this* is what I looked like at fourteen." She began to pace. "It seemed to happen overnight. One day I looked like any other adolescent girl blossoming into womanhood, the next I looked like a woman.

"The boys thought it was great. But the girls . . ." She laughed, the sound totally without humor.

Gabriel watched all that fourteen-year-old girl's pain flow into Eden's grown-up body. "I take it the girls were unkind," he commented, deliberately understating. He knew how cruel teenagers could be, especially those who felt threatened.

She picked up a knickknack from a small table then set it down. "They couldn't stand having all the attention taken from them," she told him, her voice sounding clinical and detached.

"And your grandfather?" he asked quietly.

She walked over to the overflowing bookcase. "I tried to talk to him, but he didn't care."

Her voice was still subdued. Gabriel would have preferred the earlier anger. He didn't want Eden shutting herself off from her emotions, or from him.

She picked out a thick paperback from the stacks. "So I lost myself in books. Historical romances where the hero would take the heroine out of a life of hardship into a romantic fantasy." She shoved the book back on the shelf. "When my grandfather caught me reading them, he told me they were trash and only fools read that sort of romantic nonsense."

Gabriel wanted to hold her, to wipe away her pain, but when he moved toward her, Eden went to the other side of the room to stand in front of the fire.

"I'm so sorry, honey."

She almost smiled. "What are you sorry for? It isn't anything I haven't heard a hundred times since."

"I know. People can be idiots, but to have your grandfather, of all people, dislike the kind of books you write."

She walked over and dropped onto the couch, leaning her head back as if exhausted. "He doesn't know I write them. I didn't start writing until after I left."

A light dawned in Gabriel. Was this why she was afraid to see Matt? Was she afraid he'd be ashamed of her? Gabriel resolved to ask her, but for now, he wanted to hear the rest of the story. "What caused you to leave the way you did?" he asked as he sat down on the opposite end.

She pushed her hair back from her face, her action so weary that Gabriel's heart went out to her. But he couldn't leave. Not when he'd gotten so close.

"I was miserable all through high school. Then in my senior year, I met Tommy. For the first time a boy acted as if he liked me for me. When his friends treated me like a bimbo, he defended me. Just like a hero from a book," she said self-derisively. "I told him of my dream of running away. He said he hated his folks, too and maybe we should run away together.''

Gabriel suspected he knew the ending to this story, but he stayed silent as she continued.

"We planned to leave the night of graduation. All the kids stayed out late that night, so no one would miss us until the next day.'' She looked over at Gabriel. ''You want to hear something really funny? He swore our relationship would be platonic until I thought I was ready. And I believed him. That's how naive I was.''

"I take it he made a pass?''

She smiled sarcastically. ''Not right away. He waited two whole days. And then he used every line he could think of to get me into bed.''

Gabriel could have shot himself, but he had to ask. ''Did you?''

She shook her head. ''No. And when I refused, he left me, taking almost all my money with him.''

Gabriel couldn't even bear to think of a seventeen-year-old girl on her own in a strange town with no money. ''What did you do?''

"What could I do?'' She shrugged. ''I went back to my grandfather's.''

"I'll bet Matt was livid.''

"You lose. All he said was, 'Plan to have some fun this summer. Once college starts you'll have to work a lot harder than you did in high school.' ''

"You're kidding!'' Gabriel couldn't believe any parent could be so cool.

She shook her head. "I'm not kidding. He didn't yell at me. He wouldn't even discuss my transgression. He just didn't care." Tears formed in her eyes. "I could stay or go, and he didn't care."

"Eden, no . . ."

She wiped her eyes as if furious at her show of emotion. And in spite of the fact his heart broke for her, Gabriel was glad to see it. She *did* love Matt. She'd been terribly hurt by him, but she still loved him!

He reached for her hand, but she pulled it away, crossing her arms in front of her. In spite of himself, he understood. "Did you leave again right away?"

"A month."

Gabriel winced. The hardness was back in her voice.

"On my eighteenth birthday, I became the recipient of a large trust fund my parents left me. I planned everything very carefully this time, and a few days later, ran away to San Diego. I didn't start college right away, because I thought that was where Matt might check."

This time when he took her hand he didn't allow her to pull away. "Eden, I know you were hurt, but it's been such a long time."

She looked at him, and he could see the effort she was using to keep her emotions in check.

"Yes, Gabriel, a very long time. And a lot of

things happened. Don't you want to know the rest?"

This surprised him. What else was there? He already knew about her writing. "You know I'll listen to whatever you want to tell me, honey."

"Ahhh . . ." She nodded. "But will you understand?"

Confused, he stayed silent, and she continued.

"The next year I enrolled at UC San Diego, and I met Dane." She paused, obviously waiting for a comment.

He smiled. "I never imagined you'd spent the last ten years in a convent, Eden. I have read your books, you know."

"Hmm. Well . . . I'd grown up enough that I didn't even try to delude myself that I could keep everything platonic." She looked away and tried to release her hand. Gabriel refused to let go. "Besides, I fell in love with him. He seemed so sure of himself, and I wasn't sure of anything. And he seemed to adore me." She returned her gaze to Gabriel. "Of course, I found out differently around graduation time."

Gabriel scowled. "Are you saying he didn't love you?" He couldn't believe that was possible.

Eden focused her sight on the large window across the room. Outside the storm raged. "I had just sold my first book. He had been offered a wonderful job across the country. I thought I was going with him. But he informed me that he found what I wrote embarrassing, along with my looks. The other corporate executives and their wives would never accept me, he said, and he had no intention of letting *me* hold him back.''

"That bastard!" The words were torn out of him. His fists clenched with the fury he felt. He wished that jerk was here so he could pound his face in. How could he do that to her?

Unable to sit still with the emotion that pounded like driving rain inside him, Gabriel rose and began to pace. "I knew something bad must have happened to make you dress the way you did, but I never imagined something so completely reprehensible. To take a young girl's confidence and trammel it into the dust!"

"Gabriel . . ."

He looked at Eden. "How could he not see that you were beautiful and intelligent and talented? How could he not be proud of that?" He went to stand by the fire, staring into the crackling flames, trying to calm himself.

"Gabriel . . ."

He turned on her. "And you! How could you not know? How could you let that idiot turn you into a mouse?"

"I didn't!" she protested, jumping up from her seat.

"Oh, no? Then what do you call those drab clothes you wore?"

"Walls," she said simply.

That stopped him. "Walls?"

She nodded. "Walls. That I put up to keep out prying eyes and leering grins. Walls that kept me separated from a world of men who think of a beautiful woman as a toy to be ogled and played with and tossed aside when they have better things to do." She moved closer. "Walls that I left up until I met a man worth taking them down for."

He gazed at her. At the sexy white dress that clung lovingly to her curves. At her long, shapely legs encased in sheer hose. At her hair, pulled up into a soft, becoming chignon that allowed the firelight to dance along the golden strands. At her eyes, which glowed with silver flames.

And he understood.

Without a word, he opened his arms to her. And she came into them. They held each other close.

"It's such a relief to finally know," she whispered against him.

He moved back only enough to look down into her face. "To know what, darling?"

She gazed into his eyes. "That you want me as much as I want you."

He pulled her against him and kissed her.

Eden's breath caught at the white-hot intensity of his kiss, but she met it with her own. She felt as if she'd waited all her life for this man. He was the one who'd seen through her drab garb. He was the one who'd been patient enough to wait until she trusted him, until she could finally come outside the walls.

"God, Eden, I've never wanted anyone as much as I want you," he declared against her lips, his own then trailing a fiery path down her throat.

She leaned her head back, allowing him access to every sensitive cord, every throbbing pulse point. The heat from the fire she had built earlier was like a match compared to the inferno caused by Gabriel's touch.

Longing to feel his mouth again, she turned her head to where his lips seared her shoulder. Touching his cheek, she wondered at the dry radiance of his skin which threatened to burn her fingers. "Kiss me, Gabriel," she commanded.

He raised his head to gaze at her, his expression triumphant. The light from the fire shadowed the planes of his face, making him look like some ancient, green-eyed warrior. But she was no meek maiden waiting to be plundered. She wanted him.

Winding her fingers through his thick auburn hair, she pulled him down to her, taking his lips in a kiss that would leave him in no doubt of her intentions. It only took him a moment to deepen the kiss. Together they explored, teased, tantalized, using hands and lips.

Frustrated by all the clothes between them, Eden pushed Gabriel's jacket off his shoulders. He obliged by shrugging out of it, throwing it aside. Then pulled her back against him.

As one, they sank to their knees on the plus carpet in front of the fire, undressing each other impatiently.

She worked on releasing his tie, while he unzipped her dress. He undid the back of her bra, while she unbuttoned his shirt. Fastenings unfastened, they tore off their clothes as if they were on fire.

For they were, Eden thought as she tugged off her pantyhose, on fire for each other.

Finally naked, they stopped and stared.

Gabriel reached out a hand, touching her cheek as gently as the kiss of a butterfly. "I knew you were beautiful, but I never guessed you'd be so . . . so . . . perfect," he whispered reverently.

Tears came to Eden's eyes at the wonder in his voice, because she was thinking the same thing about him.

In the glow from the fireplace, Gabriel looked like a god. Maybe Vulcan, the Roman god of fire. But no, Vulcan was much too dark, having little resemblance to Gabriel's warm personality. Maybe Apollo, the sun god, was a more appropriate comparison to Gabriel's golden tan and muscular body.

"Eden?"

Returning her gaze back to Gabriel's face, she saw his expression was almost solemn. "Is something wrong?" she asked. She didn't believe he'd changed his mind.

He shook his head. "I just need to be sure that this is what you want?"

She smiled. "You mean, am I sure I want to make love to you?"

He nodded.

"I've never been more sure of anything in my life."

With that, Gabriel scooped her into his lap and proceeded to explore the territory he had just uncovered. Eden gasped when his lips reached her sensitive nipple, arching her back instinctively. A swirling sensation filled her, causing her fingers to dig into his shoulders.

She tried to relax them, afraid she had hurt him, but Gabriel stopped her, rising up to gaze into her eyes. "Touch me, Eden, dig your nails into me, let me know you're real, not some dream goddess. I'm afraid if I close my eyes, you'll disappear."

She cupped his face in her hands. "I won't disappear, Gabriel. Not if you make love to me. Not if you make me yours."

Taking her hands, he pulled her up and led her to the couch. "Delicate skin like yours deserves more softness than a rug on the floor." Then he took his wallet out of his slacks and removed a small foil packet.

Eden raised her eyebrows, and he smiled sheepishly. "Wishful thinking" was his brief explanation.

She grinned. "A wish that's about to come true."

Her senses rejoiced when he came back to her, covering her soft body with his hard one, pushing her back into the cushions. Her skin tingled when he touched her. She pulled his head down to place millions of gentle kisses on his face and throat until his body quivered above her.

"You're torturing me," he declared when she evaded his seeking mouth. "Kiss me!"

She laughed—then resumed her teasing. "I am kissing you."

"On the lips!" he commanded, bringing up his hands to still her face. "I want to taste you, to drink from you, to fill you up." With a triumphant cry, he captured her lips, tasted them, drank from them, filling her with a yearning she'd never known before.

Her femininity burned with desire, raging with a need to be fulfilled. Her skin felt flushed with fever. A wildfire of passion heated her blood until it blazed through her veins. "Please, Gabriel, come to me," she pleaded, parting her legs for him.

Seconds later, he was inside, filling her with his own heat and passion, moving against her in a fiery rhythm. With each seething thrust her need grew more intense, with each kiss her breathing more ragged. She had no thought but him, no feeling but him, no world but him.

The lightning that flashed outside, the fire burning in the fireplace, were mere pinpoints of light compared to the red-hot fever that passed from him to her and back again, a raging circle of flame. Higher it flamed, higher and hotter and stronger until they could do nothing but explode into a million golden sparks.

Eden welcomed yet regretted the rain that would inevitably put out the fire. She'd never felt anything as intense as Gabriel's lovemaking. She'd never wanted so much, never given so much.

A small breeze from the flue wafted across her sweat-dampened body, reminding her of an autumn shower sent to cool the long, hot summer. Afraid of the cold that would come when he left her, she hugged Gabriel closer, wanting to prolong the heat, like a child longs to delay the end of summer.

hop?? ?? Gabriel *??????*, *????????? ?? ??????? ??? ????*
She *??????* *????? ?? ?????* *??? ??? ?? ???????*

_____ TEN _____

"You have goosebumps."

"So do you," she said, running her hand along
Gabriel's spine, causing him to arch against her.

Eden gasped at the intimate sensations this aroused.
"I have an idea," she said brightly.

"And what is that?" he asked, smiling.

"Let's go to bed."

"You brazen hussy! Asking a strange man to go
to bed with you."

Eden grinned. "I wouldn't exactly say you're
strange. More . . ."

He raised his brows.

"Extraordinary," she finished, earning a passionate look for her efforts.

"Thank you, ma'am." He sat up carefully. "Why

136

don't you go climb under the covers? I'll be there in a minute.''

A few moments later, Eden lay shivering in her big cold lonely bed, longing for Gabriel to come and warm her up again. What, she wondered, had ever given her the idea that she could resist him for several months? And what had given her the strength to hold out as long as she had?

It wasn't just that Gabriel was the warmest, most gorgeous man she'd ever met. He was also kind and caring. For a long time she'd thought it was just her grandfather he cared about, but now she knew that wasn't true. The whole time she'd been telling him about the past she could see that he believed every word she said.

Gabriel came running out of the bathroom and jumped on the bed. ''Let me in,'' he demanded as he slid beneath the blankets. ''It's freezing out here.''

He put his arms around her, cuddling her to him as if she was his own personal hot water bottle. His feet felt like ice against hers.

''Ouch!'' Eden cried out as she was stuck in the side by something pointy.

''What's wrong?''

''There's something . . .'' She reached down to find out what was poking her, then smiled as she pulled out another of Gabriel's foil packets. Holding it in her hand, she turned to grin at him. ''More wishful thinking?'' she asked.

Gabriel looked horrified. ''Of course not!'' His

expression changed, his eyes becoming smoldering green embers. "I just have the utmost confidence in my prowess," he drawled sexily.

"Your prowess, huh?" she said, trying to look skeptical.

He grinned. "Well, that, and the fact that I left you alone under these cold sheets long enough for you to be needing a little warmth around now."

Eden laughed. "Saying you provide a little warmth is like comparing a three-alarm fire to a firecracker."

He leaned over her, flames lit in his green eyes. "What do you say we set off a few sirens?"

She pulled him down to her. "I thought you'd never ask," she whispered against his lips before opening them for his kiss.

A while later, Eden lay happily cradled in Gabriel's arms, listening to his ragged breathing become calmer. Their lovemaking this time had been less intense, but no less wonderful. Instead of letting themselves be consumed by a fiery blaze, they had gone slowly, taking the time to get to know each other's bodies.

She now knew that Gabriel loved being kissed right below his left ear. And that sucking on his hard, masculine nipples almost put him over the edge. And she knew that she never wanted to be touched by any other man as long as she lived.

What amazed her, though, was that sometime between that first day Gabriel came into her shop and today, she had begun to trust him. Otherwise, she would never have made love with him the way she had. And she would never have told him the truth about her past.

And now, it was time to do more. She had to tell him why she had been refusing to see her grandfather.

"Penny for your thoughts?" Gabriel asked, shifting to his side so he could prop up his head. "You looked like you were miles away."

Eden looked into his beautiful warm green eyes and realized . . . she couldn't do it. She couldn't tell him. If she told him now, he would know everything, and something deep inside her, maybe some survival instinct, wouldn't let her take that risk.

"Eden?"

She smiled gently, touched by the concern she saw on his face. "I *was* miles away, floating on a pink cloud."

He grinned. "Sounds precarious."

"Not if I don't fall off," she said, knowing she was only delaying that particular descent. Because sooner or later, she and Gabriel would have to return to reality.

"I certainly don't intend to let you do that," Gabriel declared, pulling her closer. "Now go to sleep, baby. It's late."

Eden rested her head against his shoulder, marveling at how their bodies seemed to fit together so perfectly and how wonderful it was to be called "baby" in that tender tone of voice. With a brief prayer that this could last forever, she fell asleep.

Gabriel knew the moment she drifted off. Her breathing became soft and regular and she relaxed against him like a trusting child. He wished fervently that it could always be this way, but he knew the chances were slim. Tomorrow they would have to return to reality. And for him that meant pushing her to see Matt.

He wouldn't have changed this evening with Eden for the world, but he suspected it had been a mistake. Because, as much as he cared about her, there was no way he could back off about her grandfather. And he had to hope that she wouldn't get the idea that he had slept with her for just that reason.

Gabriel rested his free fist on his forehead. *God,* he thought, *I shouldn't be here!* He should have resisted the temptation. He should have waited until everything was settled with Eden and Matt. But she'd been so beautiful, so vulnerable. He'd wanted to comfort her, and inevitably he'd wanted to make love to her.

He could just imagine what Matt would think of this. *If* he knew. Which Gabriel had no intention of him ever finding out. *You were sleeping with my granddaughter the whole time you told me you couldn't find her?* he'd accuse. And what would he answer? *It just happened once, Matt. Well, twice,* Gabriel added in his head, which was starting to get one hell of a headache.

He hugged the sleeping Eden closer. *I'm sorry, baby*, he told her silently, *we can't do this again. Not until you see your grandfather*.

Feeling like a coward, Gabriel thought himself fortunate the next morning when he didn't have to tell Eden his decision. They had awakened very late, and she'd had to rush off to open the store. So, they'd barely had time for a morning kiss and a good-bye, much less a conversation.

But he'd felt less and less fortunate the closer he got to home. He had to find some way of expediting this meeting between Matt and Eden. Since he already knew Eden's side of what happened all those years ago, it was time to find out Matt's version. And how to do that without letting Matt know he had spoken to Eden?

He pulled into the sloped driveway of his house and set the parking brake. Even though he knew Matt would never question his whereabouts of the previous night and early-morning hours, suddenly he felt like a teenager who had to face his parents after staying out all night.

Matt, I have to talk to you. Matt, there's something we have to discuss. Gabriel practiced as he walked up the steps to his front door. Finding the right key, he took a deep breath and let himself in.

"Matt?" he called, closing the door.

There was no answer, so he called again as he walked through the living room to the kitchen. The kitchen was spotless and empty. Gabriel started to worry.

"Matt, are you up?" he asked, opening the older man's bedroom door.

"Of course I'm up! What kind of question is that?" Matt asked irritably from the side of the bed where he stood folding clothes into his suitcase.

Gabriel's stomach dropped. "What are you doing?"

"Packing," Matt answered, turning to the large dresser and opening a drawer.

Gabriel, trying to act nonchalant in spite of the fact his stomach was doing somersaults, leaned against the doorjamb. "Going on a trip?"

"Going home," Matt said firmly.

"I . . . ahem . . . I thought we'd already discussed this," he said calmly. He had no idea how he was going to get Matt to stay, short of telling him about Eden, that was.

"We did." Matt continued to pack. "But that was before last night."

Gabriel raised his brows. "Last night?" He was only gone a few hours! What could have happened to send Matt back to Connecticut?

"You didn't come home."

Gabriel felt guilty. It had never even occurred to him that his absence would bother his friend. "I'm sorry, I . . ."

Matt laughed. "What are you sorry for? I assume you had a great time. But my being here isn't fair to you. You don't need an old geezer hanging around, hampering your love life.''

"Is that why you're leaving?" Gabriel breathed a silent sigh of relief. This was going to be easier than he thought.

"Of course, you . . ."

"Unpack, Matt," Gabriel ordered, picking up a pile of T-shirts and putting them back in the drawer. "You're not going anywhere. In fact, forget the unpacking and come into the kitchen. I'm starving, and I have something I need to talk to you about."

"Couldn't find a girl who would feed you, huh?" Matt asked, leading the way to the kitchen.

Gabriel was happy to see the spryness was back in his friend's gait. "You're showing your age, Matt old buddy. That was a very chauvinistic comment," Gabriel admonished.

He poured them both a cup of coffee and stuck some toast in the toaster. "Sit down," he said, setting Matt's cup on the table. "Because you were so sick, I didn't press you. But you aren't sick anymore, and I need some answers."

Matt's expression was confused. "Answers about what?"

"Eden."

Matt looked up at him. "Have you found her?"

Gabriel leaned back against the counter and took a sip of coffee. "Let's just say I'm close."

"My God!" Matt whispered. "How close?"

"I can't tell you that." *Although I wish I could,*

he added silently. "I really need to know what happened between you two."

Matt set his cup down with a snap. "I was a fool, boy, a damned fool."

Gabriel's toast popped up. He put butter and jelly on the slices and brought them over to the table. Sitting next to Matt, he put a comforting hand on his arm. "I'm listening."

"You know how devastated I was when Serena passed away . . ."

Gabriel nodded.

"Well, two months later, my son and daughter-in-law were killed in an automobile accident. Eden had just turned fourteen, and I was all she had. And I failed her," he said sadly.

Suddenly not very hungry, Gabriel put down his toast. "How did you fail her?"

Matt turned his head as if to look out the window. "I'd raised a son. I knew nothing about raising a daughter," he continued. "We'd spent a lot of time with Eden while she was growning up. She was our only grandchild. But I hadn't seen her since right after Serena had died. In two short months, she'd gone from looking like a young girl to looking like a young woman."

"Why was that a problem?" Gabriel asked, although he knew the answer.

Matt turned back to him. "She didn't look fourteen anymore. Fourteen! She didn't even look eighteen! She was as beautiful and as developed as a twenty-year-old. A child I might have been able to handle, but . . .'' He trailed off.

"But in spite of looking like a young woman, technically she was still a child," Gabriel couldn't help saying.

Matt leaned back in his chair. "I know that now. But back then I wasn't thinking too straight. She didn't look like a child, and she didn't have a child's problems. We had boys calling day and night, some of them in their twenties. I think it scared her. She tried to talk to me about it, but what could I say? I wanted to lock her up and throw away the key," he finished, his voice filled with memories of those forward boys who only wanted his granddaughter's body.

"But you didn't?"

Matt shook his head, then, standing, picked up his and Gabriel's empty cups and carried them to the counter. "No, I'm ashamed to say, instead I pretty much withdrew from the situation, let her handle it on her own. Since she didn't agree to go out with any of them, I didn't worry too much. Until she started reading that romantic claptrap!"

"Excuse me?" Gabriel said. No wonder Eden hadn't wanted him to know about the novels she had written.

Matt poured coffee into the cups then brought them back to the table. "You know, those romantic novels that women read. Eighteen-year-old girls traveling round the world to marry princes, being kidnapped by sheiks.''

In spite of himself, Gabriel had to laugh at Matt's vehemence. "A little romantic fantasy never hurt anyone."

Matt banged his fist on the table. "The hell it doesn't!" his voice boomed.

Gabriel stared at him, shocked by his reaction.

"If my Eden hadn't been reading those things, she never would have run off with that stupid little jerk!"

So, he'd been right to doubt Eden's version of Matt's reaction to her running away with Tommy. Matt sounded as if he cared very much.

"Did you tell her that's why you objected to the books, that you were afraid she'd try to elope like a heroine out of the novels?"

"I didn't tell her anything." Matt hung his head. "I thought I was doing the right thing at the time, not making a big deal out of it. But I was wrong. A month later she was gone, and this time she didn't come back."

He looked at Gabriel with such despair in his eyes that it ripped Gabriel's heart out. "Do you know where she is, Gabriel? Is there really a chance I'll get my Eden back?"

For the life of him, Gabriel couldn't bring himself to lie. He only hoped Eden would forgive him. "There's a good chance, Matt."

The phone rang, interrupting him.

"I'll get it," Matt said. "I'm expecting a call. Don't you move."

Gabriel watched him walk over to the phone. Matt was taking the possibility of seeing his granddaughter again much more calmly than he had expected. He must really be recovered, Gabriel thought.

"Hello? Hello? Is anyone there?"

"What's wrong?" Gabriel asked.

Matt hung up the phone. "Damndest thing . . . If that idiot had the wrong number, why didn't he just say so?"

"Some people are just rude, I guess," he answered vaguely, but he had a feeling he knew why this particular person hadn't answered. It must have been Eden. Damn, now he'd have to stall Matt again. If she was frightened off by just the sound of Matt's voice, he didn't dare tell the older man he knew exactly where his granddaughter was. After all this time, he couldn't believe they were back to square one again.

Eden hung up the phone abruptly. Why hadn't it occurred to her that her grandfather might answer the phone? She picked up a stack of old books she'd bought from an estate and took them over to the used-book section. Coward! she berated herself. She'd spent all of the last hour convincing herself to call Gabriel and tell him why she was delaying seeing her grandfather, and now, at the merest sound of the old man's voice, she'd turned tail and run.

She started placing books on the shelf carefully, although her anger at herself made her want to throw them. Why hadn't she just asked for Gabriel? Matt couldn't possibly recognize her voice after all these years.

Her task finished, she walked back over to the counter where Amy was ringing up a purchase.

"Where's Chris?" she asked, when the customer had left.

"She had to go out for a few minutes," Amy told her.

"What for?" It wasn't like Chris to leave without telling her.

"She had something to do."

Amy's vagueness irritated Eden. "The busiest day we've had all week and she decides there's something she *has to do*? Leaving us to handle everything on our own?"

Amy looked pointedly around the empty store. "What 'everything?' "

Eden blushed. "This is just a lull. Any minute now,"

". . . hordes of eager customers could come running into the store, rampaging the place in their lust for books!" Amy finished dramatically.

Eden could feel her blush deepen. Just then the entrance bell tinkled. She turned to see who had come in, and had to laugh.

A grinning Chris pranced up to her, carrying a double-decker strawberry ice-cream cone. She offered it to Eden with a bow. "For your pleasure, Your Majesty."

Eden took the cone and grinned, looking from one young woman to the other. "You two don't fool me. This isn't for my pleasure. It's to shut me up and calm me down, isn't it?"

Amy and Chris nodded vehemently.

Eden sighed. "I apologize emphatically. I'm sorry I've been such a bitch this morning. I just have a very hard decision to make."

Chris snorted. "From the way you've been acting, I'd guess you've made and remade that decision at least a dozen times since you got here. Why don't you just pick up the phone and call him?"

Eden stared at her. "Him?" She couldn't mean her grandfather. She'd never told either of her friends that he was in town.

"Yeah, him!" Amy added. "The guy you've been gaga-eyed over the last couple of weeks."

Eden laughed. "Gaga-eyed?"

Chris leaned against the front of the counter, crossing her arms in a no-nonsense manner. "You know what she means, Eden."

Eden licked a rivulet of pink cream off the sugar cone. "All right, all right, I admit it," she said when Chris's expression didn't lighten. "But that isn't exactly the reason I've been in such a terrible mood."

A customer came in. "I'll go," Amy said, walking up to the older woman, who had a lost look on her face.

Chris returned her attention to Eden. "Whatever the reason, Eden, it's not going to do you any good to brood around here all day."

She was right, Eden thought. It was time she took herself in hand. "Thanks, Chris." She hugged her friend with her free arm. "And thanks for the ice-cream cone. I'll be upstairs. Call me if you get too busy."

"You're welcome. Just come down in a better mood, okay?" Chris said and finally smiled.

Up in her apartment, Eden sat on her bed next to the phone and thoughtfully licked at her ice cream. She told herself she was waiting to pick up the receiver until she finished her cone, but she knew it wasn't true. Knowing that Gabriel cared about her, knowing that he'd heard her side of the estrangement should make this call easy. It wasn't as if Gabriel wouldn't like what she had to say, she thought. So why was she so afraid to pick up that phone and call him?

Maybe because you're afraid that he won't find your reasons for delaying the meeting so logical, a little voice in the back of her mind told her.

Well, I'll just have to convince him, she told the voice. She picked up the receiver and dialed.

"Hello?"

Eden breathed a sigh of relief that Gabriel had answered this time. "Hi," she said.

"Hi, yourself," Gabriel answered, sounding pleased to hear from her. "How's business going?"

The ordinary question confused her. She had to think for a minute. "Business is fine. It's been busy today."

"I miss you."

Tears filled her eyes. "I miss you, too." She paused to take a deep breath. "Gabriel? I need to talk to you about something."

"Anything, my sweet," he said gallantly. She could almost hear him smile.

She tried to think how to phrase it, the right words to say, but they wouldn't come.

"Honey? Is something wrong?"

She could have cried, he was being so careful not to say her name.

Come on, Eden, it's now or never, the voice admonished, causing her to blurt, "I want to see my grandfather."

ELEVEN

Gabriel's stomach felt as if he'd just hit the bottom of the biggest dip on a huge roller coaster. "Now?" he asked, looking at Matt, who'd just walked into the room. This was more than he'd ever hoped for.

"No!" Eden's refusal came through loud and clear.

"When, then?"

"I need to talk to you. Can you come to dinner tonight?" she asked, sounding nervous.

"Dinner?" He glanced at Matt, who was motioning for him to go. "Sure, I'd like that." A thought occurred to him. "Can you cook?"

She laughed. "Of course. Would you refuse to come if I said no?"

152

He smiled. "Not a chance! When do you want me?"

It hadn't occurred to him that it was a provocative question until he noticed the silence from her end. He wondered just what she was thinking. He knew what his answer would be if it were she who asked it: "Always."

"Is seven okay?" she finally asked.

There was a lot that Gabriel wanted to say, but with Matt standing only a few feet away, he decided he'd better play it cool. "Great, I'll see you then." They each said good-bye and hung up.

"So, you have a dinner date tonight, huh?" Matt said.

Gabriel nodded. "Yup."

"Want to tell me about your mystery lady?"

"Nope," Gabriel said. "Maybe some other time. I have some stuff to do." *Like avoid Matt's curiosity.* He turned to leave the kitchen, then stopped. "I will tell you one thing, though. When you meet her, you're going to love her as much as I do."

"When do you want me?" The question Gabriel had asked, and the myriad answers she'd come up with, hadn't left her mind all afternoon. She'd wanted him the first time she saw him, she'd wanted him last night, and she'd wanted him this morning long after he'd left.

She glanced at the clock and wished the doorbell would ring. Because she wanted him now. Gabriel

Phillips was the most wonderful man she'd ever met, and she didn't want to lose him. If that meant opening herself to him, telling him everything that was in her heart and mind regarding her grandfather, then so be it.

After checking to make sure her dinner was on schedule, Eden went into the living room where she'd set a small table for two in front of the fireplace. Striking a match, she bent over to light the fire she had laid. When the kindling caught, she turned to the table and lit the candles, then stood back to admire the glow of the flickering light on the silver and china.

A perfect setting for romance, she thought. She just hoped Gabriel was still in the mood for romance after she told him the whole story and that she wanted to see her grandfather but not until her book came out.

Well, if the romantic dinner, didn't do it, she thought, surely her outfit would. The soft pink sweater she wore had a low neckline and long, full sleeves. Her wool skirt was floor-length, but she'd only fastened the top few buttons so there was ample view of her legs. She glanced in the mirror above the mantel. She'd curled her hair so it fell around her face and shoulders, making her look beautiful and sexy. That's what she wanted to be for Gabriel. But suddenly she didn't like what she saw.

What's wrong with you, Eden? You've never used sex to get what you wanted before, she told herself as she stalked to the bathroom. Gabriel would just have to be happy that she wanted to see her grandfather and accept her decision to wait for the book.

She picked up her comb and started arranging her hair into a soft French twist. That done, she bent over and fastened *all* the buttons on her skirt. She'd be damned if she was going to use feminine tricks to keep Gabriel interested. Gabriel was a sophisticated, intelligent man. He hadn't made love to her last night because of how she was dressed. He'd made love because he wanted her. She was sure of it.

The doorebell rang and Eden went to answer, feeling much happier with herself. No tricks, just straightforward honesty. She threw open the door and was struck speechless.

It wasn't fair, she thought. If she'd gone to lengths to make sure she didn't look sexy, the least he could have done was the same. On most men, the black slacks and forest-green sweater would have been fairly innocuous, but on Gabriel it should have been outlawed.

"Can I come in?"

Eden brought her gaze up to his smiling face. "Of course," she said, her voice sounding distant to her own ears.

He stepped in, took the door from her grasp, and closed it. Then he turned to her. "Can I have a kiss?" he asked.

Who could resist a smile like that? she thought. She nodded. "Of course."

They went into each other's arms. The feel of his big shoulders through his sweater, the taste of his mouth, made Eden wonder why she'd ever thought dinner necessary. Who needed steaks? She'd always wondered what characters in romance novels meant when they told their lovers they could eat them with a spoon. Now she knew. Kissing Gabriel was like eating a huge hot fudge sundae. You didn't need anything else.

He seemed to be feeling the same about her, she thought as his lips left hers to nibble at the sensitive cords of her neck.

"I'm glad you put your hair up," he said. "It makes some areas so much more accessible."

Eden smiled. So much for not being sexy, she thought.

A loud growl sounded. Eden moved back. "What was that?"

Gabriel grinned sheepishly. "I'm afraid it's me. All I've had to eat today is one measly piece of toast."

She put her hands on her waist huffily. "Is that what I do to you? Make you lose your appetite?"

He pulled her back into his arms. "Not the important one." He lowered his mouth to hers and . . .

A buzzer went off in the kitchen. Eden kissed Gabriel on the cheek, then moved out of his arms. "I guess the important appetite is going to have to wait, because dinner is ready. Go ahead and sit down." She motioned toward the table.

Gabriel's stomach growled again. "I guess I could stand to eat a little something."

Eden laughed and left the room.

"That was the best steak I've ever eaten," Gabriel said as they seated themselves on the sofa after dinner. "How did you know t-bone was my favorite."

Eden settled against him. "I figured a man your size wouldn't—"

"Eat quiche? But I love quiche."

She smiled. "I was going to say that a man your size wouldn't go in for nouvelle cuisine. You know, where you get three slices of chicken, a few green beans, and half a peach."

He nodded. "Along with some unrecognizable sauce you wouldn't feed to your cat."

"And I'd be willing to bet that when you do have quiche, you never eat less than two whole pies."

"It depends on what else I'm getting. Sometimes I only eat one—"

"—and a half!" Eden finished for him.

Gabriel had the grace to blush. "I think I'm in trouble. You know me too well."

Eden curled her legs up on the cushion. "That's okay, sweetie, I'll use the knowledge wisely."

"If that means you're going to keep feeding me steaks, I'll keep you around."

She nudged him with her elbow. "Men! All you think about is filling your stomachs."

"Oh, we think about other things, too," he said,

holding a pretend cigar, his Groucho Marx imitation particularly bad.

Eden laughed. She hadn't had so much fun in years. But the fun was about to come to an end. Gabriel had very kindly let her put him off during dinner. But she couldn't any longer.

"Eden? Look at me, baby."

She looked at him. His eyes were soft with compassion. "You know that you can tell me anything, don't you?"

She nodded.

"Then tell me what made you change your mind about seeing Matt?"

"I didn't change my mind."

He looked surprised. "But you said on the phone that you wanted to see him."

"I do." She moved away from him, to the other end of the sofa, feeling it would be easier to talk to him if they weren't in such close proximity. "I've wanted to see him, have planned to see him for a long time."

He sat forward. "But on that first day . . ."

"On that first day I'd just had the shock of my life when I read that personal ad. I hated my grandfather when I left. Hated him even more after Dane broke up with me. In my stupid, mixed-up mind I felt as if he'd put some kind of curse on me to keep me from being happy. That's why I made sure there was no trace after I left San Diego. But once I'd made a life here for myself, once the hurt from

Dane's defection had lessened, I began to miss him. He was my grandfather, the only family I had. And I started remembering the old times, when my grandmother was alive.''

Gabriel reached over to take her hand, and this time she let him.

"Matt hadn't been cold or silent back then. Serena had been everything to him. I could never take her place in his heart. But through my writing I could make a connection between us. I loved her, too. That was when I decided to write the book.''

Gabriel's grip tightened. "There's something I don't understand. If you wanted to see Matt, why didn't you contact him?''

"Because the book wasn't done.''

His brows lowered in confusion. "The book has been done for months.''

She shook her head. "The manuscript is finished. I won't go to him until I have the book in hand, complete with Serena's painting on the cover.''

"Why?''

Unable to sit a moment longer, Eden jumped up from the sofa. Just standing wasn't enough, she began to pace. It was a difficult thing to admit how dependent you were on another's opinion. But she'd sworn to tell Gabriel the truth. She stopped in front of him and took a deep breath. "Because I want him to approve of me.''

"Approve of you! He loves you, Eden. Since you left he hasn't spent a minute not looking for you.''

"And just how highly is he going to think of me when he finds out I'm Aurora Prince, author of several extremely sensual historical romances?"

"You're a highly acclaimed author, Eden, he'll be proud."

She gave him a skeptical glance. "You can't really believe that. I told you what his opinion of my reading romances was. Do you really think his opinion will be more favorable once he knows I write them?"

"Maybe not, but . . ."

"But nothing. *Serena's Lullaby* is a book he'll be proud of. I'll contact him when it comes off the press, not a minute before."

Gabriel jumped up. "But that's still six weeks away!"

"Then I'll wait those six weeks."

He shook his head. "Eden, you don't understand. When I got home this morning, Matt was packing to go home. I was able to convince him to stay, but I don't know how much longer I'll be able to do that."

Eden didn't see what he was so upset about. "I can afford the plane fare to Connecticut, you know."

"That's beside the point. He needs to see you now!"

"Gabriel, you told me he was getting well."

"He is, but with a man his age, you never know."

From his tone of voice, Eden got the feeling that he didn't believe his own words. "What does his doctor say?"

Gabriel hesitated, then sighed. "That he's fine,

better than ever." He strode over to her. "It isn't fair to make him wait another six weeks."

She threw her head back and glared at him. "Fair for him, or fair for you?"

"What is that supposed to mean?"

"Maybe you're just tired of hanging around Matt's granddaughter. Do you want to get on with your own life, Gabriel?"

"Yes!" he shouted. "My own life with you!"

Reading the truth in his eyes, she wanted to tell him that she wanted that, too. But she thought he'd understand how she felt about waiting. "So what do you expect me to do?" she asked quietly.

"Go see him. He loves you, Eden. He doesn't need a book to make him care about you."

"You don't understand. I don't just want his love. I want his approval. I need it! I needed it when I was fourteen and never got it. I needed it when I was eighteen and I still didn't have it. I don't think I could stand it if he looked at me in that cool, judgmental way of his again."

Gabriel pulled her into his arms. She tried to release herself, but he kept holding her until she gave herself up to his warmth. She laid her head against his strong chest. God, it felt good to have someone to hold on to.

"I have an idea," Gabriel said against her hair. "If it means so much that Matt see the book, why don't we just show him the galleys."

She shook her head. "That would be like giving

someone a half-finished painting or a song without a melody.''

He put his hands on her upper arms and held her away. "Eden, do you trust me?"

She looked into his green eyes, so full of honesty and caring, and had to say, "Yes."

His smile was one of relief, and Eden was touched that it meant so much to him.

"Then trust me in this, Matt does *not* need a book, even one as special as *Serena's Lullaby*, to approve of his granddaughter. He knows he drove you away. He doesn't blame you in the least."

"But he still doesn't know that I write romances, does he?"

"No, but I think you're making too big a deal of that. You aren't the only one who has grown in the last ten years. Can't you give him the benefit of the doubt?"

She turned away from him. She wouldn't have dared give the Matt she'd lived with the benefit of the doubt. But the Matt Gabriel knew seemed to be a completely different person.

But there had been another question in Gabriel's voice, "Can't you give *me* the benefit of the doubt?"

She was a fool. Gabriel had done everything possible to earn her trust. He could have told Matt he'd found her that first day, but he hadn't. He had let her go at her own pace. Even last night, when she'd been at her most vulnerable, he had refused to take advantage of her and push her about her grandfather.

And now, all he asked was that she trust his judgment.

She moved over to the sofa and sat down. She was acting like a coward in the eyes of the man she loved. How could she expect him to love her back?

She knew from the way he looked at her, touched her, that he was halfway to being in love with her already. But he couldn't love her, totally, until he respected her. And to get that respect, she had to earn it. That meant being mature and caring. That meant talking to her grandfather.

Eden hugged a throw pillow to her. She wasn't ready. She *knew* she wasn't ready. But it was possible she'd never really be ready.

Gabriel sat down next to her. "Eden?"

"All right."

"All right?"

She looked at him, at the hope on his face. "I'll see him. But not tonight—tomorrow. And I don't want to tell him about Aurora Prince yet."

Gabriel obviously didn't care. All that mattered was that she had finally agreed. He took the pillow out of her hands and, throwing it aside, pulled her into his arms. "You won't regret it, baby, I promise."

Eden wasn't so sure, but she wouldn't back out now.

Eden stood at the window, watching for Gabriel's car. She'd gotten so nervous after her decision the night before, they'd decided it might be less dangerous for the other cars on the road if he picked her up after work.

She looked down at her hands, which were red from her wringing them. This had been one of the worst days of her life. She'd been working alone in the shop, so it was just as well there'd only been one customer.

The doorebell rang, and Eden went to answer it.

"Hi," Gabriel said cheerfully. "Ready to go?"

Eden picked up her coat and purse. "I didn't see your car."

"I parked out front. You'd better put this on—it just started raining." He took the coat from her and held it out.

She slipped her arms in. "Thanks."

He turned her around, holding her coat together so she couldn't move away. "I know you're nervous, honey, but everything's going to be just fine." He kissed her briefly on the lips, then set her free. "Let's go."

Eden closed the door and locked it.

Gabriel raised his brows. "Is something wrong?"

"Since you parked out front and it's pouring down rain, I think we should leave through the shop," she said, being practical when she would rather have gone to bed and curled up under the covers.

Once they were in the car, she didn't feel any differently. After all her planning to hand her grandfather *Serena's Lullaby*, she couldn't help but feel this meeting was premature.

Gabriel reached over and covered her trembling hands with his own big, warm one. "Relax, Eden."

She glared at him. "That's easy for you to say. You aren't the one who's going to see someone you haven't talked to for ten years."

"I'm not saying it will be easy, honey. It just won't be as bad as you think."

His calm, reasonable voice made her want to punch him. He was expecting a wonderful reunion between grandfather and granddaughter. "You know, Gabriel, this reunion probably won't be all the sweetness and light you expect. I can't ignore the past, and I'm sure Matt can't either."

"I told him about your historicals."

Her eyes widened. "You what?" She couldn't believe what she'd just heard. She'd specifically told him that she didn't want Matt to know about those yet.

"I know we agreed that I would only tell him that I found *you*, but you were so worried about his reaction to your writing career that I thought I'd clear the way."

Clear the way? she thought. She was more nervous than ever. Whatever had given him the idea that telling her grandfather that she wrote historical romances would make everything better?

"I can't believe you did that."

He glanced over at her, obviously surprised by her reaction. "I thought it was best."

Eden gazed out at the rain. "*You* thought it was best? After I told you I wanted to wait?"

"Eden . . ."

"I just can't believe this! Last night you asked me to trust you, to give *you* the benefit of the doubt, and I did. Why couldn't you have done the same?"

"I was trying to make things easier for you."

"Well, you haven't! Easier would have been meeting him on equal ground. Now I have to face him knowing I am a member of the one profession he abhors!"

_____ TWELVE _____

Gabriel pulled into the driveway of a lovely brick-and-wood split-level home and turned off the motor. The rain had stopped for the time being.

"I really think you're overreacting," he said in a calm voice that to Eden sounded more than slightly condescending.

"Do you?" Eden asked coolly and reached for the handle. "We're about to find out, aren't we?" She opened the door. There was no use waiting now that she knew what to expect.

As they walked up the red-brick and railroad-tie steps, she wished she could appreciate the beauty of Gabriel's home, but her mind was filled with wondering what she was going to say to her grandfather.

Gabriel opened the front door and went in, somehow knowing she'd prefer to follow. She gave him a small smile of gratitude. This was all she could manage since her stomach felt as if it had just been invaded by every monarch butterfly that migrated to Pacific Grove, California.

"Matt's in the kitchen. We decided it would feel less formal than the living room," Gabriel commented.

Eden's lips tightened. *Gabriel* decided that Matt didn't need to see *Serena's Lullaby*. *Gabriel* decided to tell Matt about her historical romances. Gabriel and *Matt* decided that she would feel more comfortable in the kitchen. She felt as if everything had been taken out of her hands. Did they intend her to have no control at all over this situation?

"Here we are," Gabriel said, walking into the kitchen.

Eden stopped abruptly in the doorway of the large room which mixed old-fashioned coziness with the most modern of appliances. She took it in slowly, wondering if she'd ever be able to cook in this room. If things went as badly as she suspected they would, though, she might not ever see it again.

"Eden?"

She turned her head to see her grandfather, who stood next to the huge round pedestal table. Her heart started to pound. After ten years she'd expected him to look different, especially since he'd been ill. But he stood as tall and straight as the day she'd left, his expression no less forbidding.

Then he smiled. "Sit down, you two. I'll pour you some coffee."

Eden wanted to cry. How often, when she'd lived with him, had she wished for that smile, for that gentle, caring tone? All he would have needed to do was speak to her like that once, after that disaster with Tommy, and she would never have run away.

"Eden?" Gabriel put his arms around her shoulder and guided her to a seat at the table. "Come sit down, honey. And relax! Everything will be just fine," he whispered.

But she wasn't comforted. In fact, she wanted to kick him in the shin. She'd wanted to reconcile with her grandfather, but not like this, not with him in control, knowing things she was sure would disappoint him.

"Here you go," Matt said, handing her a big mug of steaming coffee.

"Thank you." She took a sip, feeling grateful for the warmth that flowed through her. But she couldn't help thinking that she would have given a lot for an ice-cream cone right then.

"I have a couple of phone calls I can make if you two would rather be alone," Gabriel offered.

"No!" Eden blushed when she realized how vehement she must have sounded. She glanced at Gabriel, whose expression showed his worry. "I'd really rather you stayed." *You wanted this, Gabriel,* she thought. *You're going to have to stay and see it through.*

Matt pulled out a chair and sat down across from Eden. "I think that's a good idea, Gabriel," he said diplomatically.

Gabriel nodded and smiled. "It's nice to be so popular," he joked.

Eden saw her grandfather's hesitant smile and realized he was nervous, too.

"Gabriel tells me you're quite a famous romance author," Matt said quietly.

Eden felt her face tighten. The first thing he says to her, and it's not, "How are you?" or "You look well," or even "I missed you." God she wanted to strangle Gabriel for thinking he knew best!

"I am an author. But I guess romance is the key word for you, isn't it?"

"I only meant . . ." Matt began.

"That I write historical romances, therefore, I can't be put into the same category as real authors?"

"Eden . . ." Gabriel said warningly.

She looked at him. "Don't worry, Gabriel. I didn't expect any other reaction—"

"Actually," Matt interrupted, "I read one of your books. I thought it was very good. The plot was quite complex, and there was no denying you did your research."

"But?"

His expression became exasperated. "No buts, Eden. You're an excellent writer. Most authors of your caliber move into mainstream. I was just a little surprised you'd stayed with the same genre for so long.''

She gave Gabriel a brief "I told you so" look, then returned her gaze to Matt. "The reason I've stayed with the genre so long, Grandfather, is because I like it. Not everyone wants to write boring coming-of-age-in-the-sticks novels.''

Her grandfather looked dismayed, but Eden couldn't bring herself to care. Why hadn't Gabriel let her wait until she could show him *Serena's Lullaby*?

The phone rang, and Gabriel excused himself to go to the other room to answer.

After he'd gone, Matt looked at her, his gray eyes apologetic. "Eden, I never suggested . . .''

"Yes, you did, by your disapproval.''

He pushed his chair back. "I don't disapprove!''

"Then you must have changed a lot in the last ten years. Back then you called the books I read 'romantic claptrap!' ''

"They were. You were a teenager. You had no business reading books like that. If I'd burned that trash like I wanted, you would never have run away.'' He took a calming breath. "But my opinion of those books has nothing to do with my opinion of your writing.''

Gabriel walked back into the kitchen, but neither Eden nor Matt acknowledged him.

"And that is?'' She glared at her grandfather.

Matt drew his lips together, as if he intended to stay silent, then brought a hand down on the table.

"That you're wasting your talent writing books that feed on lonely women's fantasies, when you could be doing something important!"

Gabriel watched Eden's warm gray eyes turn to ice and wanted to groan. How could two people who loved each other so much get themselves in such a mess? He wanted to strangle them both!

Looking like an ice queen determined to declare war, Eden rose from her chair and turned to him. "I'll wait for you in the car," she said stiffly, then left the room.

He turned his gaze to Matt, whose expression was a mixture of anger and guilt. He wasn't quite sure what to say. For the first time since he'd gotten involved in the rift between Matt and his granddaughter, he had actually been able to see in his old friend the cold, uncaring grandfather Eden had described.

Matt leaned his arms on the table. "I certainly botched that up, didn't I?" he said wearily.

Because he was feeling the same way, Gabriel felt a tinge of sympathy, but he decided not to show it. "What in heaven's name got into you, demeaning Eden's profession like that?"

"I didn't mean to say what I did, but I just can't stand the idea of her wasting all that talent on trash!"

"I don't know how you could read the book I gave you and still believe romances deserve less respect than other genres. As for your comment about feeding lonely women's fantasies, I wouldn't have believed that a man as intelligent as you could be so ignorant."

Matt looked stung. "Ignorant, am I? Are you telling me that I'm not entitled to my own opinion?"

Gabriel didn't even try to hide his disgust. "You keep your precious opinion, Matt. Shout it from the rooftops if you want. But tell me something, after spending ten years looking for your granddaughter, are you willing to jeopardize your relationship in order to expound on that *precious* opinion of yours?"

Without waiting for Matt's answer, he turned and left the room, and the house. If he couldn't talk any sense into Matt, maybe he could talk some into his granddaughter.

Eden sat near the bottom of the steps, seemingly uncaring that her coat was getting wet. With her knees drawn up, she looked very much like a lonely little girl. Gabriel sat next to her.

"I think you should go back in and talk to him, honey."

She stared off into the distance. "*You* thought I should see him before *Serena's Lullaby* was finished. *You* thought it was a good idea to tell him I wrote romances. I'm not taking your advice anymore, Gabriel."

She sounded angry on the surface, but underneath he could hear the hurt in her voice.

"Eden . . ."

She stood up abruptly. "Please take me home, Gabriel."

He stood next to her. "I don't think that's a good idea, Eden. If you'd just go in and talk to him . . ."

She turned away, but not before he saw the tears that had formed in her eyes. "You promised you'd take me home."

He couldn't bear not to touch her when she was in this state. He put his arm around her shoulder. "I know things seem black right now, but I'm sure you could work out the problems with your grandfather if you'd just sit down and talk."

She shrugged off his arm and glared at him. "That's easy for you to say. He cares about *you*! He approves of *you*! It's really ironic when you think about it. Because of you, when he looks at me all he sees is a disappointment!" She walked around to stand by the passenger door of his car. She looked over the top at him, her expression accusing. "You promised you'd take me home whenever I wanted, Gabriel."

Feeling defeated for the time being, Gabriel dug in his pocket for the keys. "You win for now, Eden. But this isn't the end of the discussion." He opened the door and flipped the automatic lock.

Without a word, Eden opened her side and slipped in. Gabriel sighed.

As they drove, a light rain started to fall. *Just the thing to brighten my day,* Gabriel thought. Suddenly, something Eden had said earlier came into his mind. "He cares about you! He approves of you!"

"Eden?"

She stared out at the rain. "Yes?"

"Do you resent my relationship with your grandfather?"

"Of course not!" she answered quickly.

Too quickly, thought Gabriel, remembering that first day they'd talked. "I guess I can't blame you. It must have been devastating for you to find out that all the love you'd wanted from your grandfather had been showered on a stranger." His speech was deliberately provoking. If this was going to be a problem between them, he wanted to get it out into the open now.

"You're damn right it upset me! Do you have any idea how it felt that day? To have you telling me how much fun you had, how he taught you to fish? Do you have any idea what I would have given for that kind of attention? To you, he was a second grandfather. To me, he was nothing more than a cold, disapproving guardian!"

Gabriel's heart rose to his throat at the pain he heard in her voice. How would they ever be able to get through this? "Baby, I'm sorry. I . . ." His apology sounded lame, even to him.

She looked over at him, her expression beseeching. "No, I'm sorry, Gabriel. I really don't begrudge you the love you got from my grandfather. I just . . ." Her voice broke. "I just wanted some of my own." She started to cry—great sobs that tore at Gabriel's heart.

As soon as he found an open parking space,

Gabriel pulled over to the curb and brought Eden into his arms. She came to him easily, holding on to him for dear life. He stroked her hair gently, letting her cry herself out.

"It will be okay, baby," he whispered, vowing silently that he would make everything okay. If he had to drag Matt over to Eden's to make this fiasco up to her, he would!

Fifteen minutes later, he parked at the bottom of Eden's steps. The spring cloudburst had ended a few moments before and a friendly wind had blown away the clouds, leaving the sky filled with stars and a fresh, clean smell in the air. They walked up the steps.

On the landing, Eden turned to him. "Thanks for the shoulder," she said, a tiny smile lightening her tear-drenched face.

He wiped the tears away. "I'm sorry tonight was such a disaster."

She nodded. "I know it wasn't your fault. Some people just have conflicting personalities, I guess."

Gabriel put his hands on her upper arms and squeezed lightly. "I know this is hard on you, Eden, but don't you think it's time you put the hurts of the past to rest. You're an adult, with a career you enjoy. Don't let Matt's opinions ruin it for you. And don't let your own pride get in the way of a reconciliation. You love Matt, and he loves you. If you'd just remember that when you're talking to him, maybe his opinions—uninformed opinions at that—about your career won't matter so much.''

"Gabriel . . .''

He put a hand over her mouth. "You don't have to say anything now. Take some time to think about it. But I hope you'll come to realize that I'm right and make peace with your grandfather, and with the past. Because you and I won't be able to have a future until you do.''

She pushed him away. "Excuse me?'' she said coolly.

He smiled, as if he hadn't heard the ice in her voice. "I love you, Eden. You must know that.''

When he reached out to hold her, she moved back, crossing her arms in front of her chest. The last thing she wanted him to do right now was touch her. "I thought I did.''

His arms dropped to his side. "What is that supposed to mean?''

"For a long time, I thought the only one you cared about was Matt. Then things began to change. It didn't matter how I dressed, you always treated me the same. And when I asked you to back off about seeing my grandfather, you did.'' That was when she'd begun to trust him, she thought, pulling her coat closer around her.

It's freezing in here. She looked toward the empty grate, remembering that night when the fire and their passion had blazed.

She turned back to Gabriel. "The night we made

love, I was sure it was because you loved me. But—''

"It was!" Gabriel interrupted.

She shook her head. "Not enough. Not nearly enough." Tears welled up in her eyes. She willed them away. "If you cared about me the way you say you do, you wouldn't be taking sides."

"Taking sides!" Gabriel exclaimed.

"Yes, taking sides, Gabriel," she returned coldly. "Why don't you just admit it? You care about my so-called grandfather more than you care about me."

"You can't really believe that!" His expression was incredulous.

Eden walked over and leaned against the back of the sofa. "I have to hand it to you, Gabriel, you're quite an actor. I could almost believe your surprise is real." Feeling restless, she picked up a small candy dish from the end table.

"Eden, that's not true," he said calmly.

So smooth, so convincing. Her need to believe him made her hands shake. She dropped the dish. The sound of china shattering seemed to release her from the icy restraint she'd placed herself under. "It *is* true!" she protested vehemently. "If you gave a damn about me, we'd have that future you dangled so conveniently, with or without a reconciliation."

Seeing the shocked expression on his face, she laughed. "Did you really think I was so dumb, so enthralled by your charms, that I wouldn't see the subtle blackmail? 'Make peace with your grandfather, Eden.' " She imitated his smooth voice. "You and I won't be able to have a future until you do."

Gabriel strode forward. "I didn't mean that!"

She smiled cynically. "I know that now. What you meant was, make peace with Matt. We won't be able to have a future."

He grasped her arms. "No, Eden! You know that's not true."

She shook him off, moving away to a safe distance. Even now, the touch of his hands made her blood race.

"I can't believe you actually think I'd try to blackmail you," he said, his voice sounding hurt. "I just don't want this rift with your grandfather to come between us."

She laughed humorlessly. "Why not? You're the one who put it there."

Gabriel stuck his hands in his pockets, his frustration clear. "No, Eden, you're the one who put it there," he countered. "If you had gone to see him that first day, we wouldn't have had this bomb ticking between us."

"That's because there wouldn't have been any *us*," she said. Gabriel wouldn't have looked at her twice if she hadn't been Matt's long-lost granddaughter.

"You don't believe that!" he protested loudly.

"Don't tell me what I believe!" she yelled back. "I'm sick of you telling me what to do. Through this whole thing, you've been the one in control. *You* held the threat of telling Matt over my head. *You* set the date for the release of my book. *You* decided that I shouldn't wait until that release before seeing him. *You* decided to tell him about my writing career. You even decided that *I* would be more comfortable in the kitchen!''

Realizing she'd almost become hysterical, she took a deep breath to steady herself. ''Do you know what I'm going to do now? I'm going to take back control of *my* life.''

''Exactly what does that mean?''

''I'm going back to my original plan. I will see my grandfather when, and not until, *Serena's Lullaby* comes off the press.''

Gabriel's eyes widened in what could have been dismay. ''But that's still six weeks away!''

''Then I'll see him again . . . in six weeks,'' she informed him, her resolve firm.

She walked over and opened the door.

Gabriel scowled. ''What are you doing?''

''I'm not doing anything. *You're* leaving.'' She couldn't stand having him here a moment longer, now that she knew where things stood between them.

''We're not done talking, Eden.''

Suddenly, she felt very weary. ''Yes, we are, Gabriel. You've made your position clear. I guess I should have seen it last night when you insisted that I see Matt in spite of the fact that I told you I wasn't ready. My feelings didn't matter. I guess they never did.''

Gabriel strode over and took her in his arms. "Baby, look at me."

She shook her head. Too tired to fight, she just stood still, willing herself not to respond.

"Eden, I do care about your feelings. I *care* about you. Maybe I pushed you into seeing Matt before you were ready, but it was only because I wanted us to be able to put all that behind us and get on with our lives."

"Please leave, Gabriel." She couldn't stand much more of this. She wanted so much to believe him. *Do you?* a cynical voice asked. *Like you wanted to believe Tommy? Like you wanted to believe in Dane?*

He stepped back onto the porch. "Why are you being so unreasonable?" he railed.

She held on tightly to the doorknob. "I've agreed to see my grandfather again, what else do you want?" she asked wearily.

"I want you!" he declared.

More than anything, Eden wanted to throw herself into his arms. *Yes, Gabriel, take me, I'm yours!* The words screamed inside her head. *Tell him the truth! Tell him!*

Eden stared up at Gabriel, his warm, handsome face and earnest green eyes illuminated by the porchlight, and felt betrayed. By his smooth talk, by his warm nature, by his caring that had turned out to be false.

When she'd tested him by keeping up her drab guise, he'd passed. But the test he'd taken today, the one it had never occurred to her to give . . . that one, he'd failed. "Make peace with your grandfather, and with the past," he'd said, "because you and I won't be able to have a future until you do." Blackmail or the truth, it didn't matter. He'd taken his side, made his choice.

"Eden," Gabriel said urgently, "did you hear me? I *want* you."

Tears came to her eyes in spite of her resolve to keep them back. "Then you'll have to wait six weeks," she said, "just like Matt."

She closed the door, a picture of his dear, shocked face and a hundred questions filling her mind. Would Gabriel still want her in six weeks? Would he love her?

THIRTEEN

Gabriel drove around a long time after leaving Eden's. How had everything deteriorated so badly? he wondered as he drove through the rain-soaked streets. Where had he gone wrong?

All he'd wanted to do was get his best friend and his granddaughter back together, so he and Eden could get on with their lives. And now Eden was refusing to see Matt, and *him*, for six weeks.

Well, I'll tell you one thing, Miss Eden Pendleton, you may be able to get away with this with Matt, but I'll be damned if I'll go a month and a half without seeing the woman I love! Gabriel declared silently, hitting his fist against the steering wheel for emphasis.

God, how was he going to tell Matt? *What* was

he going to tell Matt? He couldn't tell him about *Serena's Lullaby*. Eden would never speak to him again, after that fiasco with the other books.

When another fifteen minutes of driving around didn't afford him the answers he sought, he became resigned. He was going to have to face Matt eventually, he thought. It might as well be now. So, when the sky opened up for the third time that night, he headed home.

Once there, he found Matt where he'd left him, sitting at the kitchen table. But he knew the old man hadn't stayed put the whole time. Like his granddaughter, Matt was a pacer.

"Is Eden okay?"

Gabriel nodded, joining his friend at the table. He would have given a lot for a nice cold beer right then—several, in fact. But the alcohol would only cloud his already clouded mind. No, his best bet was to remain sober.

"What are you afraid of, Matt?" he asked.

The older man's expression became confused. "What do you mean?"

"For ten years you've searched for your granddaughter. For ten years, you've waited to make up for your neglect. You had her right here, and you as much as sent her away. Why?"

"Because I think she's wasting her talent, that means I'm afraid of something? Come on, Gabriel," Matt said, his disgust clear.

Gabriel leaned back in his chair, resting his ankle

on his knee casually. But he didn't feel casual. "We're back to your precious opinion again, I see."

"Eden's my only grandchild. All the dreams I had for my son were transferred to her when he died. That's why I pushed her so hard to do her schoolwork."

"While her life was falling down around her ears," Gabriel couldn't help commenting.

"She had some problems—all teenagers do. She would have been happier once she got to college. In fact, from what I hear, she *was* happier once she got to college."

Matt had broken off abruptly, and Gabriel had a feeling he knew what the older man was thinking. Knowing it might hurt him, but needing to get everything out into the open, he voiced it. "And away from you."

Matt winced. "Do you think I don't know that? I know what I did to her."

"Then why didn't you learn from your mistakes? Why make such a big deal out of her choice of career?"

"Because I love her! Because I want her to be happy."

Gabriel shook his head in wonder. He couldn't believe Matt still couldn't see he'd been wrong. "And you don't think she could possibly be happy writing historical romances?"

"Instead of something worthwhile? How could she be?" Matt asked seriously.

Gabriel narrowed his eyes at Matt. There must be some way to get through to him. The books! he thought, letting his chair drop with a snap. "I'll be right back," he said.

"Gabriel, where are you going?" Matt called after him.

"I'll be right back."

Gabriel found a small cardboard box in the hall closet, then went to his bedroom. Standing in front of one of the three overflowing bookshelves, he began to take down book after book. All Eden's.

The box nearly full, he walked back to the kitchen. "I have a present for you," he said, dropping it on the table.

Matt stood up. "A box of books?"

Gabriel nodded. "A box of Eden's books."

"What am I supposed to do with these?"

"Read them," Gabriel said blithely.

Matt's eyes widened. "All of them?"

"Uh huh."

"And why would I want to do that?" Matt asked.

Gabriel raised an eyebrow. "To prove you're right?"

Matt laughed a little. "Or wrong?"

Gabriel grinned.

"And just when am I supposed to do all this reading?"

"During the next six weeks," Gabriel told him, crossing his arms in front of his chest. Here goes, he thought.

"Six weeks? Why six weeks?"

"Because you're going to have plenty of time."

Matt looked at him suspiciously. "And why is that?"

Gabriel took a breath. "Because Eden refuses to see you until then."

"What?" Matt roared.

"Eden . . ."

"I heard what you said! What the hell is going on here?"

Gabriel pulled out a chair and sat down. It was getting harder and harder to act nonchalant about all this. "You can't be all that surprised after what happened earlier."

"I thought she might take some persuading, but . . . six weeks? Can't you talk to her?"

Gabriel shook his head. "It won't do any good."

Matt sat down next to Gabriel, his face filled with dismay. "What am I supposed to do until then?"

Gabriel grinned, picked a book out of the box, and handed it to Matt. "Read?"

"Are you sure I've told you everything?" Eden asked, shifting through some order forms.

"Yes, for the fifth time," Amy said with good-natured impatience. "You've told me everything I need to know, not to mention several things I don't need to know. Now, quit worrying!"

"I can't help it. I haven't been away from the store for this long since I opened it."

"Then it's about time you had a vacation." Amy grabbed Eden's arm and pulled her out of the chair. "So, get going!"

Eden laughed. "It *is* a working vacation, you know."

"If it'll put you back on an even keel, I don't care what it is. Chris and I are going broke buying you ice-cream cones," she said dramatically.

Eden put her hands on her hips. "I beg your pardon? I've reimbursed you for every one!"

"Right," Chris chimed in from the door of the office. "All three hundred and twelve of them."

Eden picked up her purse and jacket. "I can see I'll get nothing but abuse if I stay here."

"Seriously, Eden," Amy said. "I wish you'd tell us where you're going. I'm not worried about the shop, but what if something happens to you. A woman traveling alone . . ."

"I'll be fine," Eden said. "I promise I'll check in every few days. I just don't want anyone to know where I am." She hated to do this to her friends, but if she stayed, she knew she wouldn't be able to keep away from Gabriel, or keep him away from her.

"Eden?"

She brought her attention back to her assistants.

"What about Gabriel?" Amy asked.

"What about him?" It took all the strength of will Eden could muster to keep the emotion out of her voice.

"What if he calls? What are we supposed to tell him?" This time Amy's impatience was anything but good-natured.

"Tell him . . ." She shifted her purse onto her shoulder. "Tell him he set the terms." She turned and walked out of the office.

"Eden!" Amy called after her, obviously wanting an explanation for her cryptic statement.

Eden opened the front door. "I'll be in touch in a couple of days. 'Bye." She closed the door and hightailed it to her waiting car. The sooner she got out of Portland, the better.

"Thanks, Bob. No, no, I understand. Don't worry about it." Gabriel hung up the phone, leaned back in his chair, and sighed. Three full days of phone calls and schedule shuffling and all he'd been able to cut was two weeks. Two lousy weeks!

Oh, well, he thought, at least it was better than nothing. Picking up the receiver again, he dialed Eden's number. After one ring, there was a click, Eden's metallic message on her answering machine, and a beep.

"I'm tired of you not picking up. We have to talk. I'm coming over," he shouted into the phone. He'd stayed away from her for three days, a major concession as far as he was concerned. He'd had enough.

Fifteen minutes later, Gabriel drove into Eden's alley, planning to park next to her car. But her car wasn't there. He scowled and drove around to the front. Maybe Amy or Chris knew where to find her.

There were no customers in the store when he went in. At the ring of the bell, Amy walked out of the back room, stopping abruptly when she saw him.

"Hello, Amy," he said politely, wondering why she looked as if he'd caught her with her hand in the cookie jar.

"Hi, Gabriel." She walked up to stand behind the counter.

"Is Eden here?"

Amy shook her head. "No, she's not."

"Will she be back soon?" he asked. Why was Amy being so quiet! Usually she didn't stop talking.

"I'm afraid not, Gabriel."

He scowled. "What does that mean?" There was something strange going on here.

"Eden's gone," Amy blurted.

"Gone? Gone where?" he shouted. Had she run away again? He couldn't believe she'd leave everything she owned and take off.

Amy smiled. "Don't worry, she'll be back," she said wryly, as if she'd read his mind. "She's gone on a research trip."

Irritated at Amy's lack of information, Gabriel shoved his hands in his pockets; otherwise he might be tempted to strangle some answers out of her. "And just where did this research trip take her?" he asked with studied patience.

Amy bit her lip. "I don't know."

"You don't know," he said vaguely, then more loudly, "What do you mean you don't know?"

"Don't yell at me, Gabriel. She said she didn't want anyone to know where she was."

"When did she leave?"

"Tuesday."

She sure didn't waste any time, he thought. "And you have no idea where she might have gone?"

Amy shook her head. "It could have been anywhere. She did call this morning to say she'd arrived and that everything was fine."

So at least she was okay. "Did she mention me?" he couldn't help asking.

"Not today."

He let out a sigh of relief. "Then she did leave a message for me."

Amy nodded. "Sort of."

"Sort of?"

"Before she left, we asked what we were supposed to say to you if you called. And she said to tell you . . ." Amy hesitated, biting her lip again.

"Tell me?" Gabriel raised his brows. When she didn't answer right away, he became impatient. "Tell me *what*, Amy?"

"That you had set the terms."

What the hell did that mean? "Is that all?" he asked.

Amy nodded. "I'm sorry."

"Did she say when she'd be back?"

"Six weeks."

Six weeks. And he had no way of telling her he'd moved the publication date up two weeks.

Six weeks. He'd had no intention of staying away from her so long. It seemed she knew it, too. Otherwise she wouldn't have run away.

But there was a difference this time, a voice said. This time she intended to come back.

He set the terms. What did that mean? He thought back over their conversation of a few nights ago. She'd been so angry at him. *He set the terms.* What *terms*?

"Oh, my God!"

"Gabriel, are you okay?" Amy looked alarmed by his outburst. "What's wrong?"

"Nothing, Amy." He leaned over the counter and kissed her cheek. "Not one thing! Thanks for the message. I'll see you later." He ran out the door.

Showered and dressed, Eden opened the door of the steamy bathroom and shivered. The rest of the small beach cabin that had been her home for the last month felt as frigid as a mid-winter's day. She glanced at the fireplace, which was filled with the cold, dead ashes from last night's fire, and contemplated starting it up. It was evident from the wind whistling through the tiny crack under the front door that the southern coast of Oregon had not yet learned that winter had ended long ago and it was nearly summer.

Not that she should complain, she thought as she

went into the kitchen and poured herself a cup of hot coffee. The fact that the summer came late to this part of the coast was the only way she'd been able to rent a house just a stone's throw from the rugged coastline. Every night she fell asleep to the sound of the waves pounding against the rocky beach.

She placed two pieces of wheatberry bread in the ancient toaster and pushed down the lever. It really wouldn't be worth building a fire yet, she decided, since she would be out most of the morning. She'd light one when she got back from the library.

The toast popped up. She spread the two pieces with some of the local blackberry preserves and placed them on a small plate. Picking up a cloth napkin, she took the toast and coffee over to the small table by the window so she could look out over the windblown sands and crashing waves.

But it wasn't the beauty of the stormy sea that filled her mind this morning. It was her grandfather. In another two weeks she'd be facing him again, and in spite of the fact that this time she would have *Serena's Lullaby* in hand, the very idea scared her.

During the past month, she'd gone over the conversation she'd had with him again and again, trying to make sense of it. Trying to figure out how what had been meant to be a reconciliation had deteriorated so badly. Although the time and circumstances hadn't been her choice, she'd wanted to be there. Yet, she had left. Not only left, she'd run away.

Gabriel had said she was an adult and that her

grandfather's opinion of her career shouldn't make that much of a difference. What he didn't seem to understand was that she felt like it was *she* Matt disapproved of, not her writing. It had been that constant nagging at her choice of clothes, her choice of friends, her choice of reading materials that had driven her away. They had been her choices, and because her grandfather had felt they were bad, she thought he was saying *she* was bad.

Something her grandfather had said came into her mind: "If I'd burned that trash like I'd wanted, you would never have run away."

Suddenly she was awash with memories from her adolescence. Her grandfather looking embarrassed during the summer when she'd been sunbathing on the lawn, and yelling at her to put some clothes on. Her grandfather refusing to let her go out on dates until she was sixteen, and then grilling the few boys she had dated. His comments when he'd picked up one of her novels to find the heroine was a sixteen-year-old girl who had left her family to follow the soldier she loved into the war between the states.

To her teenage mind, his words had been shattering, showing her how much he hated her. But he hadn't hated her, she thought, staring out at a little patch of blue that had appeared in the cloudy sky, and remembering how worried he always looked when she left on a date. Not, as she'd thought, as if he expected her to do something wrong, but, just maybe, as if he was afraid she might get hurt.

Eden glanced at her watch. The library opened at nine, and the head librarian had promised her access to the archives that held much of the recorded history of the area, especially of the sailing ships that had crashed on the rocks during the last century. She had better go now if she wanted to make it in time.

She finished her breakfast and went out to the car. But all the way into town, other memories followed her. Memories of her grandfather saying, "If Serena was here, she wouldn't let you dress like that. If your dad could see you, he'd have my hide." She'd been so involved in her own loneliness, in her own problems, it had never occurred to her that Matt had just felt out of his element.

And now that it has, a cynical voice in her brain chided as she stopped the car in front of the library, *are you sure it's true?*

I don't know, she told the voice, *but it's worth thinking about.* After all, he'd only raised one child, her father. And no matter what anybody said, raising boys and raising girls are two very different things. That could be why he was so much more comfortable with the young Gabriel than with his own fourteen-year-old granddaughter, who'd developed the body of a twenty-year-old.

Maybe he hadn't been cold underneath. Maybe it was his discomfort, and her imagination, that had made him seem that way.

But if all this was so, she thought as she walked into the building, why hadn't he told her? Why hadn't he just been honest with her and told her he had no idea how to raise a girl, that he might need her help?

She had so many questions that needed to be answered. And if things worked out the way she wanted, in two weeks she'd have the answer to every one.

"Good morning, Miss Pendleton," the head librarian greeted her. "Eager to get started, I see."

"Good morning, Mrs. Scott." Eden smiled at the older woman who had been so helpful with her research. "If the archives have the information I need, I could be finished today."

Mrs. Scott picked up her key ring. "Come this way. School's in session, so you'll probably have the whole library to yourself this morning."

Several hours later, in spite of the fact her stomach was growling unmercifully, Eden skipped down the library steps. She couldn't believe the wealth of material that had been hidden in that dark back room. But there'd been everything she needed. Now, all she had to do was compile her notes into some semblance of order, and she could start on her new book. For the first time since she started *Serena's Lullaby* she felt terrifically inspired.

After grabbing a bite to eat at the local deli, she headed back to the cabin. When she got there, the wondrous sight of the sun streaming through the dark clouds to shine on the gray-green water drew her down to the beach. Who wanted to stay indoors on a glorious day like this?

Picking her way through the long grass and driftwood, she made her way down to the sand, then to the water's edge. She stood for a moment, watching the waves and thinking of the day she'd driven over to the coast with Gabriel.

While she walked just above the waterline, she thought about him. But that wasn't unusual. During the past month, Gabriel had been ever with her, just at the back of her mind, whether she was working or walking or thinking about Matt. She knew he must be furious with her, running away like this. But she could deal with his anger.

What she could no longer deal with was having Matt between them. He had only been stating the truth when he'd said they couldn't have a future until she put the past behind her. Although she'd resented his saying it at the time, during the long night that followed, she'd come to believe he was right.

That was why she had decided to go away. But she also knew if she told him before she left—if she saw him—that she'd lose her nerve and stay. And they would fight. Because on waiting until *Serena's Lullaby* was published to see her grandfather again she would not change her mind.

But Lord, she did miss Gabriel. They'd only had one night together, yet her bed seemed big and empty without him. Food seemed tasteless when she couldn't look up and see him sitting across from her.

She stopped when she reached the cliff that cut this beach off from the next cove. Bending down, she picked up a stick and threw it out over the water. Even the few days they'd had sun here had seemed bleak and cold without Gabriel there to tell her how the light on the water sparkled like her eyes.

Wiping away tears caused by the wind and by her thoughts, Eden turned back toward the direction of her cabin and resumed her walk. In the distance, she saw another beach walker coming toward her.

The way the man walked, with long, easy strides, reminded her of Gabriel. *Chin up, girl,* she told herself. *Just two more weeks to go. Don't go letting your imagination run away with you.*

But the image of Gabriel only grew stronger as the man drew closer. The color of his jacket was the same as the one Gabriel had worn on their ride to the coast. Even the way he had his hands shoved in his pockets reminded her of Gabriel.

The sun came out from behind a cloud, painting the beach gold. Eden stopped. The stranger's dark hair suddenly glowed with red highlights.

Eden began to run.

FOURTEEN

When Eden halted, so did Gabriel's heart. But it started to sound again when she began to run. Because she was running toward him, not away as he'd half feared.

He stopped, taking in the glorious sight of golden blond hair whipped by the wind and the most beautiful smile he'd ever seen. But she never slowed down, and he barely had time to brace himself for the impact as Eden hurled every inch of her nearly six-foot body against him.

"Gabriel, oh, Gabriel!" she cried. "I couldn't believe it was you." Then she kissed him.

Not even during the night they'd spent together had she kissed him with such intensity. But now her mouth clung to his as if her very life depended on it. His head began to swim, and he forgot everything—his anger, his loneliness, his fear, everything except his love for her.

"Eden, Eden. I've missed you so much," he murmured when her lips left his to scatter kisses across his face.

"Shh, Gabriel, don't scold me now. Just kiss me."

He didn't have to be asked again as he reclaimed her lips, crushing her to him. He explored and tasted, tasted and explored, reveling in the velvety warmth of her mouth.

He ran his hands over her, longing to feel the firm softness of her body, but her thick coat impeded his quest. Impatient, he slipped his hands between their bodies and unzipped the offending garment.

As needful as he for contact between them, Eden pulled at the snaps on his jacket, then slipped her hands under his sweater. She moaned when her fingertips touched the warm skin of his back just as his found her sensitive spine.

His mouth burned a path down her throat while his hands continued to explore her back. Deftly he unhooked her bra, then brought his hands forward to cup her breasts. The sensations he reaped with his strong, tender touch made her want to drag him down on the windblown sand and make mad, passionate love to him while the seas crashed and the storm howled around them.

The thought brought her down to earth with a jerk. "Gabriel . . ."

"Let me love you, Eden. I want you so much," he murmured against her neck as his hands continued to wreck havoc on her senses.

"Gabriel, stop! Please!"

The urgency in her voice brought his head up. "What's wrong?"

She tugged his hand and tried to pull him up the beach. "Come on!"

He didn't move. "Eden, what's wrong?"

"Look, you idiot!" She pointed to the water that had been whipped into a frenzy by the coming squall. Even as they hesitated, the sea was gathering its forces, as if readying for attack. "We have to move. Now!"

This time he didn't resist, instead taking the lead and hauling her up the sand to higher ground. Once there, they turned to watch the wild waves submerge the patch of sand where moments ago they had almost made love.

Gabriel gazed at Eden, his eyes filled with awe now that they were out of danger. "I think you saved my life."

Eden smiled nervously as she refastened her coat. "It's too early for thanks. You might drown yet. It's about to start pouring," she yelled over the howling wind. "We'd better get inside."

As if on cue, the sky opened up, and the two lovers ran for shelter from the storm.

Finding the rocky path to her cabin, Eden scrambled up it as fast as she could, with Gabriel following close behind. Once at the top, they scurried across the small yard to jump onto the covered porch.

"Whew! I thought we'd never make it," Gabriel said breathlessly, brushing the excess water from his jacket.

Looking out at the tempest they'd just come through, Eden registered that Gabriel's car was parked behind her own and wondered, as she hadn't when they'd been occupied with other things on the beach, how he had found her.

She turned to ask him and began to laugh.

"What's the matter now?" he asked, sounding mistreated.

"You look like a drowned cat," she commented between giggles.

"Just remember that cats have nine lives, young lady. Now, open that door," he ordered. "It's freezing out here."

She dug the key out of her pocket and opened the door.

Once inside, she took off her coat and shivered. She should have started that fire earlier, she thought. It was barely warmer in the house than it had been outside.

Gabriel doffed his coat and hung it on the back of a kitchen chair. "I'll build a fire. You go get us some towels. Oh, and get out of those wet clothes while you're at it."

"Yes, sir!" Eden saluted.

He slapped her on the behind as she passed him.

"Don't get smart with me, young lady. You have a lot of explaining to do."

Eden went to get the towels. There were a few questions she was interested in hearing the answers to herself.

In her bedroom, Eden took off her wet things and put on a thick pair of socks and a black sweat suit with a turtleneck collar. It wasn't the most romantic outfit, but at least it was warm.

By the time she wrapped her hair in a towel and gathered up a couple for Gabriel, he had the fire blazing. But he was nowhere to be seen, and his jacket was gone.

The front door was pushed open and Gabriel came in carrying a large leather duffel bag.

Eden raised her brows. "Planning on staying a while, were you?"

He didn't grin like she expected. "No, as a matter of fact, I was headed home today if I couldn't find you."

The thought that he might not have come, that it might have been another two weeks before she saw him again, brought a lump to her throat, and she thanked God that he *had* found her. The interlude on the beach had brought home to her more than anything could have how much she missed him.

"How did you find me?" she asked, trying to keep her voice nonchalant.

"It wasn't easy, let me tell you. When you decide

to disappear, you sure do a hell of a job," he said wryly.

She turned her gaze to the fire so her eyes wouldn't give away just how glad she was to see him. The scene on the beach had proven without a doubt that he wanted her physically. But they had a lot to talk about before she could be sure he'd also welcome the love she kept safe for him inside her heart.

Once she felt secure enough to look at him, she immediately felt guilty. "You're soaked. You must be freezing. Why don't you go into the bathroom and change? You could even take a hot shower if you want."

His eyes blazed emerald-green fire. "Only if you'll take one with me," he said, his voice low and sexy and much too tempting.

"No, thank you," she answered too quickly. She felt the heat come to her cheeks and wasn't totally sure it was all due to embarrassment. "I'll fix us some coffee and something to eat while you're changing."

He grinned and left the room.

After putting on a pot of coffee and fixing a tray of snacks with the cold cuts and French bread she'd bought at the deli earlier, Eden moved the small coffee table and old chintz love seat closer to the fire. Then she went to find some candles. The sound of the wind rattling the doors and windows promised a long and stormy night. It probably wouldn't be too long before the electricity went out.

Candles placed in various containers, she scattered them around the cabin, then went to curl up on the couch and wait for Gabriel.

A moment later, the bedroom door opened and he walked out. "Thanks. I feel much better," he said, coming around to sit beside her.

He *looked* wonderful, she thought. She breathed in the fresh, clean scent of him. He'd changed into another pair of jeans and a green sweater that matched his green eyes almost to perfection. His hair was still damp, and she had to physically restrain herself from reaching up to touch the curls that had fallen onto his forehead.

He narrowed his eyes at her. "That was a pretty clever message you left with Amy," he commented.

Not quite knowing how to reply, Eden busied herself pouring him a cup of coffee and handed it to him.

"So, you did get it, then," she said.

He smiled wryly. "It took me a few minutes. Didn't Amy tell you?"

She took a sip from her mug. "All she said was that you'd left seeming much happier than when you came in."

"It's a good thing she didn't see me a few days later when I could find no trace of you. I was far from happy then."

"Sorry about that," she said, sure she didn't sound in the least sorry. She'd needed this month away to sort out her feelings for him. She hadn't wanted to make the same mistake with Gabriel that she'd made with Tommy and Dane. "So, how did you find me?"

"A couple of weeks ago, I remembered a conversation we once had about the plans for your next book. You said something about basing the story on the sailing ships that wrecked on the rocks in southern Oregon. All I had to do was figure out which town you'd decided to do your research in."

She smiled at his resourcefulness. It was awfully nice knowing that he had listened to her so closely. She picked up a piece of French bread from the plate and handed it to him, then took one for herself. "So, you've been traveling around looking for me for two weeks?" she asked, not seriously believing that he would have.

"I'm afraid not, darling. Only the last couple of days. I do have a company to run, you know."

She stared at him with awe. While he'd been talking he'd put together the biggest sandwich she'd seen since Dagwood in the comics. "When was the last time you ate?"

He grinned. "Breakfast. Besides, looking for runaway girlfriends makes me hungry."

"Had a lot of them, have you?"

He shook his head, too busy chewing to answer out loud. "Only you," he said when he finally swallowed.

Once he'd finished his sandwich and three cups of

coffee, he stood up and headed for the bedroom. "Wait here, I have something for you."

He came back a moment later, a plainly wrapped parcel in hand, and sat down. He gazed into her eyes with such intensity that she couldn't have looked away if she wanted to. "This past month has been the worst in my entire life. Not being able to see you, to touch you, has been torture. Not having any idea where you were was agony for me. Believe me, if this had been ready I would have been here two weeks ago when I finally had an inkling of where you might be. I love you, Eden."

He placed the package in her hands. "Unwrap it."

Eden held her breath as she undid the string and tore off the brown paper. She finally let it out when she held *Serena's Lullaby* in her hands.

"Oh, Gabriel, it's here. It's finally here." She looked up at him. "But how? I thought it wasn't due out for another two weeks."

"While you were making plans to run away . . ."

"I didn't run away!" she said indignantly.

"Whatever . . . While you were making plans, I was making phone calls and taking meetings, and rearranging schedules, anything I could to get the production date moved up. But all I could manage was two weeks."

Tears filled her eyes at the effort he'd gone to. "Oh, Gabriel, I love you." She threw herself into his arms and kissed him with all the love and passion she'd been keeping for him all her life.

And he kissed her back, letting her know without a doubt that no matter what happened in their lives they would always be together.

When both were satisfied with what they'd found, they parted, secure in the knowledge it would only be temporary.

"When I found out you'd gone, I was furious," he told her, then smiled indulgently. "But then Amy gave me your message. 'She said to tell you that you had set the terms.' It was clear Amy had no idea what it meant. Then I began to think, 'What terms?' And suddenly it occurred to me. You'd been so angry at me. Why? Because I'd told you we couldn't have a future until you made peace with your past."

He gazed at her with such love she thought her heart would burst. "You hadn't gone away to avoid anything or run away, as I'd first thought. You went away to work for us, didn't you?"

She nodded, tears blurring her vision. "I had to make peace with myself and with my past. When I fell in love with you, I realized I'd made even bigger mistakes with Tommy and Dane than I'd thought. I'd never really loved either of them. So with you, it was important to be sure about my feelings before I made a commitment to a future with you."

He smiled. "And you are sure, aren't you?"

Her gaze went over his handsome, confident face. "Oh, yes. I love you with all my heart, Gabriel Phillips, always and forever."

"And I love you, my darling Eden Pendleton."

He gave her a quick kiss on the lips. "Which reminds me. You didn't say if you liked the book."

"Of course I do," she exclaimed, looking down at her grandmother's painting on the cover. "It looks beautiful, just like we planned . . ." She faded off, looked up at Gabriel, then back at the book. "It has my name! It doesn't say Aurora Prince."

Gabriel smiled. "Do you mind?"

"Mind?" She gazed at him, eyes wide. "Of course I don't mind. But how? Why? What will this do to sales for your company? No one's ever heard of Eden Pendleton. Gabriel, I really appreciate this, but . . ."

He put his fingertips on her lips. "But nothing. You wrote an exceptional book and you deserve the credit for it."

At that moment, Eden felt more loved than at anytime during her entire life. "My grandfather was the only reason I kept my real name a secret. Now that he knows, you can use both names in the promotions."

"We'll work it out, Eden. Now, quit worrying."

"Okay." But silently she vowed to make sure that Gabriel's company didn't suffer because of this gesture. "What did Matt say about the book?" she asked, keeping her tone nonchalant while butterflies played baseball in her stomach.

"Nothing."

"Nothing?"

"He hasn't seen it yet," Gabriel explained.

"Oh." She lowered her head to look at the book. Matt still didn't know. "I thought you might have given it to him the minute it came off the press after the way I left again."

"Baby, look at me." He put a finger under her chin and lifted it until she looked him in the eye.

His expression was so tender and full of love that Eden almost gasped.

"This book is your gift to give, Eden. I wouldn't take that away from you."

The tears that she'd been holding in check began to flow, and he gathered her into his arms. But comfort wasn't what she wanted right then. She drew back to look at him.

"I love you, Gabriel, with all my heart and body and soul. And I've missed you so much." She pulled his head down to hers. "I want to make love with you," she murmured against his lips, placing tiny kisses against them. "I can't wait until everything's settled with my grandfather. I promise I'll make peace with him. But I need you now. Please love me."

"Oh, Eden," he said huskily, as if he held back tears of his own. "*You* are the most important thing in my life. Even if you had run away from Matt again, I would never have let you run away from *me*. I need you too much."

The lights went out at that moment and the storm increased its rage outside, but she barely noticed as

Gabriel took her into his arms and showed her the paradise that their future together promised.

In spite of a long night spent in the midst of a passionate tempest, they rose early for the long ride back to Portland. Gabriel had to be back at work the next morning, and now that she had the book, Eden wanted to see her grandfather.

They arrived back in the city late afternoon and drove straight to Gabriel's.

"Is that you, Gabriel?" Matt called from the living room when they opened the front door.

Gabriel smiled at Eden and squeezed her hand. "Everything's going to be fine," he whispered.

She smiled back. "I know."

They walked into the large living room, which had a beautiful view of the city below. But Eden only noticed it briefly as her gaze went to her grandfather, who rose from the club chair where he had been reading. He still held the book in his hand.

His eyes widened when he saw her. "Eden!"

"Grandfather, I . . ."

"No, don't say a word. I was wrong. This is one of yours." He held up the book. "Gabriel gave me a whole box of them. This is the last one I have to read. I thought books like these were frivolous pieces of fluff, full of sex and little else. And I was embarrassed to find out you wrote them."

Eden winced, holding tight to Gabriel with one hand and *Serena's Lullaby* with the other.

"But I was wrong," he continued. "It's clear that you put a lot of intelligence and thought in your books, not to mention the accuracy of your research. And I'm so sorry I hurt you. Can you ever forgive me?"

Tears formed in her eyes at the look of contrition on the face of her proud grandfather. "I can forgive you," she said, "if you can forgive me."

He opened his arms for her. She gave the book to Gabriel and ran to her grandfather.

"I was so afraid of losing you, all those years ago, that I think I was afraid to love you," he whispered against her hair. "I loved Serena with all my heart, and she died. I loved your father, and he died. You were all I had left, and deep down, I was afraid the same would happen to you."

She hugged him tight, feeling a little guilty that none of this had occurred to her.

"I was a fool, my little Eden. It took this last month to show me how much of one. Serena and my son didn't die because I loved them. And you left because of my actions, not because I loved you." He gazed down at her face. "And I do love you."

"I love you, too, Grandpa," she said, using the name she'd used as a child. "And I have something for you."

She walked over to Gabriel, who handed her the book, and kissed him on the cheek. Then she turned back to Matt.

"I wrote this for you, as a peace offering." She handed him the book.

He looked at the cover and read, *Serena's Lullaby* by Eden Pendleton. Tears came to his eyes and he swallowed. He touched the painting on the cover. "This is one of Serena's. Eden, I . . . don't know what to say."

"Just tell me you're proud of me. That's all I ever wanted."

His head jerked up. "Proud of you? I've always been proud of you. How could I not be? You're beautiful, intelligent, successful. When you were little, you were the funniest little imp." He gazed at her, his expression filled with all the love and pride she'd always longed for. "And you're talented. All those other books, and now this. God, yes, I'm proud of you."

Eden ran to him, throwing herself into his embrace. "Now, I have everything I ever wanted," she whispered.

He drew back to look at her face, then looked over at Gabriel. "Why do I have a feeling you're talking about something other than your foolish old grandpa?"

Eden blushed as Gabriel walked over to join them.

"Matt, I've been wanting to ask you this question for weeks."

"What question?" the older man asked.

"I'd like to ask for your granddaughter's hand in marriage." He took a blue velvet box out of his pocket and opened it.

Eden gasped. Inside was the most beautiful diamond engagement ring she'd ever seen.

Gabriel took her left hand in his and looked at Matt. "Well?"

He smiled. "I can't think of anything I'd like better. But I think the answer is up to her."

Gabriel drew Eden to him. She felt breathless and excited and so very very happy. They'd already planned to spend their future together, but it had never been put in these specific words.

"Eden Pendleton, I love you with all my heart. Will you do me the honor of marrying me?" he asked, his voice filled with love and hope.

"Yes!" she cried, throwing herself into his arms. "Yes, yes, yes!"

He hugged her so tightly she thought he'd never let her go. Then he set her away. "Wait, it's not official yet." With that, he put the ring on her finger. "There," he said. And they smiled at each other.

"Ahem." Matt cleared his throat. "Can I get in on this?"

Eden and Gabriel laughed. Gabriel shook his friend's hand and hugged him. Then it was Eden's turn.

"You really are happy, aren't you, Edie?" he asked, using her childhood name.

She nodded.

"I know Gabriel is the right man for you. You look peaceful, like you've found your paradise."

"I know one thing," Gabriel said, putting his arm around her waist. "I've found mine."

FIFTEEN

Gabriel left the bookstore and walked across to the park, enjoying the feel of the sun after the morning's rainstorm. Stopping in the rose garden, he bent to smell one of the summer-blooming roses and marveled at how much sharper his senses seemed to have become in the last month since he and Eden had gotten married. *I guess that's what being in love does to you*, he thought.

A movement caught his eye, and he stood to watch his newly wedded wife sail by him, back straight, eyes ahead, just like the first day they'd met. He smiled. She was even wearing the same oversize trench coat and knee-high black boots, but he knew that underneath, instead of a drab skirt and blouse, she wore the short denim skirt and hot pink T-shirt they'd bought on their honeymoon in California. And instead of being stretched by a tight bun, her hair floated around her shoulders like a golden cloud.

She was also carrying a double-decker strawberry ice-cream cone.

Uh oh, he thought. Something must be up. Eden used ice cream the way other people used a drive in the country or a cup of tea, to calm her nerves and help her think. I wonder what's going on.

He followed her to her favorite bench across from the small grove of fruit trees, knowing she liked watching the birds that flitted among the branches. By the time he joined her, she'd taken off the coat. He was glad he'd persuaded her to buy that outfit. She looked young and carefree, as if she didn't have a problem in the world. And he meant to keep it that way.

She didn't turn her head when he sat down, but he knew she knew he was there.

"Hi," he said.

"Hi."

"Ice cream good?"

"Wonderful," she said matter-of-factly, then continued lapping at the pink ice cream.

She certainly didn't sound like anything was wrong. But how could he tell if she wouldn't even look at him?

"I saw you here that first day," he said.

She stopped licking. "What?"

"The first day we met, when you closed for lunch."

That got her attention. She looked at him, her rain-colored eyes wide with curiosity.

"You followed me?" she asked.

He shook his head. "No, you were so stubborn I needed to cool down. I thought a walk in the park would help. You walked right by me and sat on this bench. I was sitting over there." He pointed to a nearby spot.

She blushed. "So you saw . . ."

"I saw you transform yourself into the most beautiful, innocent woman I'd ever seen. That's why I didn't call Matt. You weren't the cold, angry woman I'd seen in the bookstore after all. I had to try to get to you."

She grinned. "You got to me all right."

He took her hand. "And you got to me. I love you with all my heart, Eden."

Her lovely face flushed with pleasure. "I know. I love you, too."

He ran a finger along her cheek. "Then you must know you can talk to me when you're upset."

She looked away. "What makes you think I'm upset?" she asked, then started to lick her ice-cream cone with a vengeance.

"Well, the ice-cream cone for one. And the fact that you didn't throw yourself into my arms for another. Did I do something to make you angry?"

She sent him a telling glance. "Of course not."

He hadn't really thought so. They hadn't had anything even close to a fight since their time at the beach. But he was still getting to know his beautiful wife.

Maybe it was her grandfather. "Is it Matt?" he asked. "I know he had a doctor's appointment this morning, but when I went by the bookstore, Chris said he'd gone to lunch with my father. He would never have put himself through that if he wasn't feeling well."

"Matt's fine," Eden said.

Gabriel would have been surprised if she'd said anything else. Since he and Eden had reconciled, Matt acted twenty years younger. He'd moved into Eden's apartment above the shop and had even taken over some of her management responsibilities so she could work on her new book.

"Then it must be *Serena's Lullaby*. I know you've been nervous about it, but there's no need. The book will do great."

"It's not the book," she said calmly, then took a bite of the sugar cone.

Tired of playing twenty questions with his wife and getting nowhere, he became exasperated. "Then what *is* it?"

She still wouldn't look at him. "Matt isn't the only one who had a doctor's appointment this morning."

Gabriel's stomach dropped. "Are you sick? You never said anything, honey, I . . ."

She touched his hand gently. "I'm not sick. At least, not technically."

"What does that mean?"

She popped the rest of the cone in her mouth, chewing it thoughtfully, then grinned. "We're going to have a baby."

"*What?*"

"*We* are going to have a baby." Eden couldn't stop grinning. When the doctor had told her the test was positive, she'd been stunned. For some reason the idea of pregnancy had never occurred to her. And even if it had, she would have disregarded it. Except for the one time at the beach, Gabriel had always used protection, even after they'd married. But as the doctor said, "It only takes once."

She looked at Gabriel, whose expression was as stunned as hers must have been earlier.

"A baby?" he asked quietly.

"Uh huh."

"But we . . ."

She smiled. "Uh huh."

His expression changed, as if a light had dawned. "Except that one time . . ."

"Uh huh."

He gazed at her, his gorgeous green eyes as bright as emeralds. "Then it's true?"

She nodded, tears forming in her eyes. Somehow, telling Gabriel made it all the more real. They were really going to be *parents*.

He hugged her to him. "Eden! My God!" He held her away. "Are you sure?"

"Very sure," she said, smiling through her tears.

He ran his gaze over her as if expecting her to look different. "Are you okay?"

"Healthy as a horse," she reassured him.

He laughed. "I can think of better descriptions."

She threw up her hands. "Pregnant three minutes, and already my descriptive powers are shot to hell."

Gabriel put a finger to his lips. "Shh, the baby might hear you and come out cussing."

Eden laughed. What fun they were going to have, she thought.

"By the way, did you say 'pregnant three minutes?'" Gabriel asked, a mock serious look on his face. "When is this baby due anyway?"

"I might have been exaggerating a bit," she told him. "The baby is due late spring."

"Just about a year from when we met," he said with a secret smile that nonetheless told her he was thinking about that meeting and wondering at the outcome.

His expression changed, but this time there was nothing false about his seriousness. "Are you sorry about it happening so fast? I know we discussed having children, but we haven't had very much time for just the two of us."

Eden stared at the fruit trees across the way. It wasn't hard to imagine their son or daughter darting among the trees, playing hide-and-seek. Was she sorry? Not on your life. She could hardly wait.

She turned back to gaze at her husband. "You've brought me more happiness than I'd ever imagined I could have. It might have been nice to have you all to myself a while longer, but having your child, knowing that our love made this tiny being growing inside me, only adds to that happiness. I adore you, my darling Gabriel."

An emerald fire lit his green eyes, rewarding her for her declaration.

"What about you, my husband, are you happy about the baby?" She knew the answer, but wanted to hear the words.

He took both of her hands in his, holding them gently. "When I saw you in the park that day, I saw a promise of paradise under the cold exterior you tried to project. When I stood with you before the minister and we said our vows, I knew I had finally been invited inside to share that paradise with you. You and I having a child completes our paradise. I have everything I need."

Seven and a half months later, on a beautiful spring day, Matthew Gabriel Phillips was born. And every night, like her grandmother and great grandmothers before her, Eden put him to sleep with the lullaby she had heard as a child.

Hush, little angel, close your eyes.

The heart of the Lord is tender and wise.
He gave you parents full of love.
As long as the stars sparkle above
Who'll watch over you, awake or asleep,
and love you as much as the oceans are deep.
A heaven on earth His kindness has brought.
Remember the love that He has taught.
Hush, little angel, close your eyes,
And dream of the promise of paradise.